Englishwoman

at

Christmas

By Jenny O'Brien

By Jenny O'Brien

Ideal Girl Trilogy
Ideal Girl
Girl Descending
Unhappy Ever After Girl

Englishwoman in Series
Englishwoman in Paris
Englishwoman in Scotland
Englishwoman in Manhattan
Englishwoman at Christmas

Short Stories
Englishman in Blackpool,
(Prequel to Englishwoman series)
Dunkirk - Rescuing Robert

Anthology
12 Days of Christmas

For Children
Boy Brainy

Praise for Jenny O"Brien

"This author has a true gift. All her books are easy reading with a story to tell that keeps you wondering what next". Booklover Bev via Amazon.

"I absolutely adored this story. It was fun, flirty, romantic, tragic, emotionally heart-breaking at times but also very heart-warming." Adele for "Kraftireader" book blog.

"This is a lovely little story which I really enjoyed". Elaine Fryatt, via Amazon.

"Another wonderful, romantic cosy read beautifully written with warmth love and tenderness". Michele Turner, via Amazon.

"A beautiful little English romance". English Rose via Amazon.

"She captures the reader from the first paragraph, engrossing them with her heroine"s journey of love and loss, to the very end". Susan Godenzi, writer.

"A really nice read". Sue Parkinson via Amazon.

"Really enjoyed this book, couldn't put it down. Now on the third book in the series". Susie G via Amazon.

To the twins, with love xx

'I dream things that never were: and I say 'why not?'
George Bernard Shaw

Chapter One

Belgravia
Christmas Eve

'But sir…'

'It's alright, it's the very least I can do. After all, it is Christmas Eve.'

'Well, if you're sure?' Parker paused on the threshold, one hand on the door. 'Are you sure you wouldn't like to reconsider? Christmas alone, when you could be…'

'That will be all, Parker. I haven't forgotten the invitation but I'm in no mood for company.'

'Yes, sir. The hamper is still in the boot,' his voice holding a degree of uncertainly at the thought of leaving any task undone. 'And remember there is snow forecast for later.'

'You and your weather warnings. The last time you gave me a scare like that all we had was a couple of miserly snowflakes. Now off with you before I change my mind. I'll catch up with you in a few days,' he added, with a smile. 'You'll find a little something for you on the hall table.'

Oliver Ivy, the fifth Earl of Worton, climbed into the front of his black Jaguar and slammed the door shut before adjusting the mirror in addition to the car seat. Parker was quite a bit shorter than his six-foot three. But height wasn't the only way he differed from his chauffeur as he started fiddling with the radio station. It might well be Christmas Eve but if he had to listen to another rendition of *Fairy-tale in New York,* he'd scream.

It wasn't that he was a humbug, he thought, as he tuned into Radio Four. Even last year he'd made a special effort and had managed to gain some degree of enjoyment from the company of friends. But that was last year and so much had happened over the last few weeks to dim any hint of festive cheer.

He could still recall that as a child he'd loved this time of year. His mother used to decorate Worton Abbey from top to toe with bunches of fresh holly, tied together with red velvet ribbon. They'd used the same ribbon to hang up their stockings above the mantelpiece in the second drawing room; three identical stockings but with very different gifts. His mother's always contained diamonds while his father's bulged with the largest Cuban cigar to be had. His gifts changed year on year from brightly coloured lumps of plastic to small and educational until they'd finally stopped…

His hand paused on the dial as he wondered where that memory had come from. He hadn't thought of those Christmases in years but now he could almost smell the light scent of his mother's perfume as she knelt down beside his bed to press that one, last, sweet kiss against his childish cheek. If he closed his eyes, he felt sure he'd wake up again in his bedroom with Batman wallpaper and his large comforter, which invariably ended up on the floor for him to trip over.

It had all been a long time ago; a time before boarding school and a time before bereavement. Fifteen was too young to lose one parent but to lose both and in such dreadful circumstances…Every December after he'd been packed off like a parcel to stay with distant relatives who'd done their best with a surly depressed teen but, by then, Christmas had long lost its sparkle. He'd dampened down those memories with an iron fist. Now, for some reason, on this Christmas Eve, they'd all come flooding back when he'd least expected them, or indeed wanted them.

He sighed. Must be all that forced exposure to Christmas music but, whatever the reason for the memories, they were unwonted and unasked for. Instead of Christmas holly berries and the memory of his mother's kisses, now all he craved was peace and solitude and the odd glass of whiskey to dull his thoughts. No, he didn't want to dull them. He wanted to rip them asunder and shred them to pieces. If he lived 'til he was a hundred he'd never forget the look on Joey and Janey's parents' faces. They blamed him and weren't they right? The buck stopped at his feet, his fingers tightening around the steering wheel.

Pulling into the street outside his Belgravia apartment block, he noted the heavy, cloud-filled sky even as the first flakes of snow started landing on the windscreen with a vengeance. It had been snowing on and off all day and a white Christmas was now a cert, not that it bothered him. He had his evening planned down to the last minute and whether or not it snowed was immaterial. He had food, warmth and music, in addition to a bottle of Chateau Mouton-Rothschild 1963 and a Cuban cigar larger than a banana. He wasn't really a smoker. In fact, he hadn't had a cigar since last Christmas but it was just something he did once a year just like his father and his father before him. Perhaps this year he'd leave it in its wrapper. Perhaps, after recent events, it was time to move on and make some new traditions. Perhaps...

Driving along Marble Arch, the streets empty of all but the hardiest of dog walkers, he noticed the first sign of the persistent snow that Parker had predicted clinging to the edges of the pavement and, for the first time, considered the wisdom of driving himself in this weather. He laughed out loud at his own stupidity. It wasn't snow that was the problem. This snow was as fresh as a new-born lamb. It was when it froze later he'd have to worry and by that time, he'd be tucked up safe.

He pulled into the underground carpark and, grabbing the brightly wrapped bottle, made his way to the lifts and then on up to the top floor. This was a party he really couldn't get out of. Indeed, the medical director had told him that his career was on the line if he failed to attend this, the last party of the year.

Well, that was a joke for a start, a bitter taste in his mouth. What career? His career was in the same place as his self-esteem and self-belief. He'd blown it, despite being the only one in the world capable of performing such complex surgery. He hadn't touched a scalpel since and he was starting to wonder if this was the end of his illustrious career. His eyes jerked to his hands and the persistent shake that seemed to have taken up permanent residence in recent weeks. He'd been drinking too much, far too much. It hadn't taken Parker's disapproving stare to tell him. He was an adult but for some reason, he could only sleep at night after the level on the whiskey decanter drained to zero.

He wouldn't drink tonight, only something soft until he could sneak away and hibernate until it was all over.

It was horrendous. He'd known it would be bad but barely-dressed women cavorting with balding blokes really wasn't his idea of fun as he declined yet another glass of fizz from the hands of yet another pouting pretty with more lipstick than sense. Stuffing his hands in his pockets, he headed across the room. It would almost be worth getting hitched just to wipe the smug smiles off their faces although what woman would look at him now?

His mouth pulled into a thin line. He'd managed to avoid matchmaking mothers and their increasingly desperate daughters for the last thirty-six-years - with a bit of luck he'd manage for the next thirty-six. Being rich, titled and famous had its drawbacks but marriage to the wrong woman held many more.

Chapter Two

Bond Street
Christmas Eve

'**W**ell, I'll be off now.'

'Oh, yes. Thank you, Clare.'

'You do realise it's four pm, four pm on Christmas Eve, don't you?'

'Is it? Already? Sorry. That meeting earlier really set me back. I'll finish off here and lock up,' she said on a smile. 'Off you go and have a lovely day with that man of yours.' she added, standing up before dragging Clare Wakelin, her right-hand woman, into a deep hug. 'Oh, wait a min. I have a little something for you.' She stepped away and, leaning over the desk, finally found what she was looking for under a pile of drawings. 'Sorry, its only money I'm afraid but...'

'Money is fine, thank you. Here.' Clare reached behind her back and withdrew a parcel before pushing it into her hands. 'I bought one for myself and thought you might like it. Mind you don't open it until tomorrow though,' she said with a final smile, pulling the door to a close.

Holly looked up from the present, her fingers gripping the squishy gift for dear life even as she felt something in her heart shift, not that she was meant to have a heart, her lips narrowing. Or, at least, that's what the last man she'd been on a date with had accused her of. His parting comment, shouted through the letterbox, of her being a heartless frigid bitch was something that would live with her forever.

Perhaps he was right, although deep down she knew that wasn't the case. She cared. She cared perhaps too much, which was why she'd armour-plated her heart after that one time - the one time she'd let someone in and they'd tried to smash her to pieces.

She placed the package next to her bag with a gentle hand being as it was the only present she was likely to receive. Sitting back behind her desk, she pulled the drawing towards her with a sigh. The interruption, although a welcome one, had broken her concentration and now, instead of seeing preliminary sketches for Lady Nettlebridge's African Ballroom, all she saw was a picture of her on her wedding day. Not that any pictures existed; she'd destroyed them all. The only thing she had left from that day was her wedding band, something she'd kept in an act of defiance.

Eighteen years was a long time and memories of that day were hazy at best. She couldn't even remember what he looked like, not really. She remembered he was blonde and blue eyed and she remembered what he'd done or what he'd tried to do and she'd never trusted another man since. How could she when she'd loved him with everything she had, only to find he didn't really love her at all? She had been a lousy bet, a thrill and finally, the thing that hurt the most, a meal ticket.

Of all the things she'd taken from her marriage, her wedding band and her wariness of the whole of the male species were the most useful. Her clients were mainly female but they came with husbands, partners, lovers. A casual arm thrown across her shoulders, stray fingers brushing against her breasts, a thigh pressed too closely as they discussed flooring and lighting. If she'd been single she'd have been vulnerable but there was always the shady figure of a husband in the background to fall back on.

The pencil snapped in her fingers. But instead of reaching for another, she threw the bits aside before resting her head in her hands. Four o'clock on Christmas Eve and here she was; still at work when she should be at home in the bosom of her family. The only problem was that she didn't have one, not even a miserly cousin or aunt – no one.

For the first time in years, she wondered what it was all for. Yes, she was a successful business woman having built her design empire from the money her father had left her. She had premises on Bond Street and was invited to all the best parties with all those beautiful people that appeared across the pages of Hello and OK magazine. The phone was a hacker's dream filled as it was with the private numbers of the great and the good. But she couldn't count even one of them amongst her friends. She had no friends and, until early this afternoon, she'd had no family.

Raising her head, her gaze landed on the envelope, the buff envelope from Messrs. Pike, Pidgeon & Prue and, peeling back the top, she tipped out the contents even though she now knew them by heart.

The envelope contained three items; a slip of headed notepaper with an address somewhere in Cornwall and, right down the bottom in a mass of metal, a bunch of decidedly dodgy looking keys. But it was the last item that scared her most, the last item she'd left exactly as she'd found it; a second envelope, faded with age and written from the grave. Did she want to know about this Martha Branch, the woman who'd abandoned her? There could, after all, be a thousand reasons for her desertion but not one that she could ever forgive her for.

Shifting her attention she ran a fingernail along the smooth edge of the heavy, scrolled-metal of the largest key as she tried to imagine what kind of door it belonged to, not a prefab two-up-two-down semi, that's for sure. It had to belong to something old and intriguing. Something brick built and made to last as her eyes flashed to the address and her lips mouthed the words.

Forever Cottage
Polruan
Cornwall

Even the word held mystery and intrigue tangled amongst the letters. Cornwall; closing her eyes she tried to sum up images of the place, a place she'd never been. There'd be blue sea, sand and Cornish teas but that's all her tired brain could come up with as her gaze came to rest on the keys again and a thought popped into her head.

Why not find out?

Cornwall was only a couple of hours away. She could pack a bag and the contents of the fridge in no time and, instead of enjoying the deserted delights of Christmas Day in the metropolis, she could be wandering along the shoreline with the wind in her hair. The cottage was hers and, if Mr Pidgeon was to be believed, it still had all the amenities switched on. He'd assumed, sitting behind his ancient desk that she'd want to sell it almost immediately. He'd assumed so much, too much. He'd assumed, for instance, that she'd actually known she'd had a mother to start with, the skin puckering around her mouth. He'd assumed she'd known of her whereabouts but had just chosen not to visit and she couldn't be bothered to put him out of his misery as she remembered his frank stare. She'd stood up from the brown, bentwood chair before shaking his hand and wishing him goodbye. She didn't bother with wishing him anything else, why should she? He'd be heading home to Mrs Pidgeon to enjoy the start of Christmas while she had to come to terms with having a mother who'd never bothered to buy her a birthday card, let alone a present. He could think what he liked. The cottage was hers; that's all he needed to know.

She collected up the drawings before stuffing them into a folder just in case she felt like continuing to work on the designs. It wasn't likely but she might just find the inspiration she needed from the edge of a sandy beach. Slipping her black cashmere coat across her shoulders and her bag over her arm, she made her way to the door, her four inch heels tip-tapping across the parquet flooring.

Later found her opening the door of her new apartment. It was a little upmarket for her with its concierge service but her business was doing well, better than she'd ever expected and, to come home from a long day in the office to such luxurious surroundings, was bliss.

As apartments went, it was of the square, impersonal type she so despised. But once through the door, there was nothing impersonal about it. Everything in the room echoed her distinctive sense of style and rhythm as London's most go-to interior designer. The walls were painted in a rich clotted cream and interspersed with antique, gold-framed mirrors reflecting the tasteful artwork dotted around the room. She was a lover of big, chunky pieces and, designs by Moorscroft vied for pole position with quirky Clarisse Cliff and the thick bronze influences from the *Art Nouveau* period. Whilst each object was unique and original in its own right, the combination of eclectic pieces against such a stark backdrop of muted creams was startling.

Flinging her coat across the back of the sofa, she stepped out of her shoes before phoning the chauffeur service she used. She'd checked the flights before leaving the office, booking herself on the last one out of London City Airport and, with a spurt of speed she should just about make it. Padding into her white bedroom and through to the walk-in wardrobe, she started rummaging through rails upon rails of suits and dresses, each one plain, un-patterned, tailored and black. A widow's wardrobe if ever there was one. But she wasn't in mourning, far from it.

Setting the wheels in motion to annul her marriage the day following her wedding had been the right thing to do. Something she'd never regretted for a second. His actions had made her brave, so brave that she didn't care what she did next. On the morning after, when she should have been in the grips of post-wedding night euphoria, she'd had the sense to ring both her solicitor and then the travel agent. She'd spent the next two weeks in Italy rebuilding her new life from scratch. When she'd returned, she'd returned, not to Wraysbury but to London and she'd worn black ever since.

Scrabbling around the bottom of her wardrobe wasn't something she normally had to do but she knew she had a pair of jeans somewhere…Jeans, t-shirts, jumpers, boots. She ran over the list in her head with a smile as she stuffed the items into her leather holdall along with a handful of underwear, and her serviceable PJ's and towelling dressing gown.

Food came next. Picking up another bag she headed to the kitchen and proceeded to empty the contents of her fridge; milk, smoked salmon, French mayonnaise and champagne but no turkey. She added her favourite bread and then finally, tea, coffee and some dried pasta along with a selection of cheeses and crackers, which should do her until the shops opened again after Boxing Day.

Wishing the concierge a very happy Christmas, she hurried down the steps, pleased find the car waiting for her. Not her usual but a Jaguar would do just fine as she tapped the window with her gloved hand.

'My bags.'

'Your bags?'

He'd got out of the car and was now standing in front of her, the frown of all frowns piercing his brow. It was obvious he wasn't happy at having to turn up this late on Christmas Eve but tough. She was paying through the nose for the service and she'd even planned on giving him a hefty tip, a tip he was about to lose.

'Yes, my bags - if you wouldn't mind putting them in the boot? I'm on a tight schedule.' She snapped, glancing at her watch. 'I have to be at London City in under the hour.'

'Airport?'

'Yes, man. The airport.'

God, she really had a thick one here. Was it really that difficult a request? It wasn't as if it was a long journey or anything. Ignoring his continued stare, she wrenched the back door open and collapsed into the rich leather seat.

As a driver, he wasn't up to much but she couldn't complain about the car. Her usual driver, Claud, had only fabric-covered seats that seemed to retain the smell of all the previous bodies that had ever sat on them. Whereas the back seat she was sitting on now smelt of leather, overlaid with a hint of some subtle aftershave probably from the last man to hire the vehicle.

Chapter 3

Oliver looked from the woman to the bags in something akin to bemusement until his brain shifted gear, and his hand stretched up to feel the outline of Parker's chauffeur cap, which he'd propped on top of his head in a fit of madness. He'd only stopped outside the apartment block to drop off the hamper before taking the car around to the underground carpark. He had no other plans than a date with his book, bottle and then bed and certainly no plans that included a trek across London on the behest of some stranger. But, what the heck, it was Christmas Eve after all and it wouldn't hurt. In fact, it would probably reduce his hangover somewhat if he started a little later.

He placed her bags next to the Fortnum & Mason's hamper and made his way to the driver's seat but not before he'd checked her out through the back window.

She wasn't as young as he'd first thought. In her thirties probably and with skin that rarely saw the sun. He couldn't make out much more; his eyes automatically travelling down to her left hand, now free from the gloves she'd worn, and then he lost interest. Yes, he was a man with the usual male appetites but not for whey-faced women; whey-faced married women.

He couldn't remember the last time he'd driven across London and in the snow too, probably never. In truth, it was madness he was even driving at all. Oh, he had his driving license but just never got the chance to get much practice in. It wasn't that he wasn't capable; it was just every time he reached for the car keys the look of intense disappointment on Parker's face soon had him returning his hands to the safety of his pockets. When he'd inherited the earldom on the death of his father, he'd also inherited Parker and whilst he enjoyed, more than anything, revving his Porsche through the streets, apparently it wasn't *the done thing* for a middle-aged earl.

Pulling out of the unloading bay, he raised an eyebrow at the different type of night he was having. He'd decided on a nice bottle of claret to go with the Sirloin steak resting in the fridge, all eaten on a tray in front of the TV. He'd given the housekeeper the week off and slobbing about in his dressing gown and slippers without the threat of any untimely interruptions was all he desired. And now he was pulling onto the M23, which was already covered with a sprinkling of snow and his tyres were starting to feel decidedly slippery. He checked in his mirror before starting to overtake an oversized mobile home, reassured by the car's recent service in addition to the four-wheel-drive nature of the vehicle that Parker, for some unknown reason, had insisted upon. It's not as if he got to do much off-roading in and around Belgravia.

His eyes strayed from the road to the mirror briefly, after all, he had a stranger in the back of his car and even he'd heard not to pick up hitchhikers. She was resting back against the brown leather seat with her eyes closed and suddenly he wanted to know what colour they were. He also wondered what the mad dash to the airport was all about. Where was her husband for instance, or partner, or was she shooting off to some last-minute festive family gathering to meet them all? Maybe she was meeting someone at the airport, a lover, her partner? Maybe she was flying out somewhere exotic for some last minute Christmas sun just like he'd done last year.

God that was a holiday he'd be happy to forget forever. A week on Grand Cayman all on his own strolling along Seven Mile Beach, a beach populated by couples and families on the holiday of a lifetime. He felt like an intruder, a gate-crasher. He shook his head slightly and the thought dissolved. He'd much rather be here, now, driving in what was proving to be the worst weather conditions, with some strange woman in the back than strolling along some sandy beach where he hadn't felt welcome.

'We're here madam,' he said, parking the Jaguar in front of the airport entrance. He leapt out and held the door open with a differential smile, or at least he hoped it was deferential; it might look as if he was suffering from wind. But it was the best he could do in the circumstances. It would be just his luck to meet someone he knew, dressed up as he was still wearing Parker's cap. What a lark, he might even take to the streets late at night to see if he could moonlight as a cabbie, although perhaps not, as an image of him on the front page of the tabloids popped into his mind.

Starting to unload her bags from the back, he felt a sudden pressure on the top of his arm.

'Hey, sorry mate. We're just about to close the airport. No flights in or out until Boxing Day so unless you want to sit here until then, I suggest you make tracks.'

'What was that—?'

They both turned to look at his passenger as she walked over to join them.

'I was just telling your chauffeur the airport is closed, the snow, you know.'

'God, what am I going to do now?'

Oliver caught the eye of the porter and shrugged his shoulders. If ever there'd been a washout of an evening, this was it, he thought as he reloaded the bags before opening her door and helping her inside.

Sitting again behind the wheel he turned in his seat. 'That's unfortunate. Where to now, madam?'

'Cornwall.'

'Cornwall?' He stared at her in disbelief and it must be said a fair bit of amusement. 'You'd like me to drive you to Cornwall in these weather conditions, not forgetting that it's Christmas Eve? It will take hours.'

'Only about four and I'll make it worth your while.'

'How much?' The words slipping past his lips before he had time to engage his brain. Was he seriously considering driving all that way and in these conditions? But what else was he going to do with his evening, a little voice interrupted; the same voice that forced him to push his whiskey bottle aside each night. The same voice that usually only came up with the most sensible of suggestions. This wasn't sensible. This was stupid.

'Three-hundred?'

'Make it five-hundred and it's a deal.'

If he could recall the words, he would but her small nod and even smaller smile told him that it was far too late to turn back that particular clock. It wasn't the first time his brain had allowed his mouth to get him into trouble but it usually didn't necessitate going hours out of his way. He'd berate himself later about what a complete and utter fool he was but now he had an eight hour round-trip to embark on. It was his turn to smile. He'd find some hotel in Cornwall and instead of spending Christmas alone in London, he'd spend it holed up in the poshest of hotels. But for now, he'd show her he was the best driver she'd ever had as he returned to the boot and removed a rug before opening the door and placing it over her knees.

'Here you go, madam. You might as well be comfortable. It will be a long journey. Do you have any preference as to which route?'

'The quickest.'

'Where exactly in—?'

'Polruan. It's somewhere on the coast.'

He wanted to ask what, or indeed who, there was in Polruan, clearly a place she'd never been that was so urgent as to make a dash across the south-west coast corner of England in the ever-increasing snow, but he didn't. Instead, he fiddled with the satnav and, with a quick glance over his right shoulder, pulled out into the now deserted street and towards the M4.

Chapter 4

Two hours later and the situation was getting to him. Staring into the snow hammering down against the windscreen and in a car he was only used to driving for more than a couple of miles at a time was unnerving to say the least. It was all the more unnerving to be sitting in front of someone that hadn't spoken a word since her last comment about the route he should take.

Apart from the odd shuffle from the back, he might as well have been driving alone. She'd even forced him to turn off the radio so now the only sound to be heard was the noise of the wind and the scrabble of the tyres as they resolutely tried to retain their grip on the increasingly slippery road. The large noticeboard up ahead, reflected in the lights from his headlamps, had never been more welcome. Glancing at the fuel gauge he clicked on his indicator and started pulling into the right-hand lane.

'Why are we turning off?'

'I need to get petrol, madam. Are you warm enough?' he added. 'Would you like me to pick you up something - a coffee, a sandwich?'

He would've liked to have asked her whether she needed to use the facilities but he didn't feel his chauffeur skills were quite up to the mark in that regard. He was obviously in a subservient role here and Parker would rather die than ask such a personal question.

But he needn't have worried. 'No, I'm fine,' there was a slight pause. 'Thank you for asking.'

It was a relief to stretch his legs as he unfolded his frame from the car and made a good attempt at being knowledgeable as to the location of the petrol cap. Visiting petrol stations was something he hadn't done in years, probably not since university if he was being honest. Whilst he liked to think he took care of himself, really his life was run by all the people in his employ. All he had to do was get up in the morning and go to work and he hadn't even managed that for the last three months. In truth, he was a pretty useless individual and the one thing he'd been good at, he now couldn't do. He even had to hold the petrol nozzle between both hands to ensure he didn't shake fuel all over the forecourt.

But, standing filling up the tank while the wind and the snow swirled around him, he made himself a silent promise. After tonight he'd make a concerted effort to get his life back on track because if he could drive hundreds of miles in these conditions, surely he could pick up a scalpel without his hand shaking?

'Would you like me to pay?' He started and, tilting his head, noticed she'd rolled down the window.

'No that's fine. It's on me. Are you sure you wouldn't like—?'

'No, I want to get down to Polruan as quickly as possible.'

So do I, but instead of adding voice to his thoughts, he just nodded before making his way to the shop.

'Tea or coffee, or there's water?' he said, holding out two cups, even as he noted her sharp glance.

'Tea then, although I thought I said I didn't...?'

'But I do. I need something to keep me awake and it would be rude for me to drink alone. There are also sandwiches in the bag; cheese and tomato or ham. They only look as if they're made of plastic. I'm sure they taste...'

'Horrible,' they rang out in unison, her tentative smile lighting her face to something akin to beauty. And suddenly he had an urgent need to see what colour her hair was underneath that hat. Her eyebrows were faint brown but that meant nothing these days, although she didn't look as if she'd covered herself in make-up, not like those women at the party who'd layered it on with a trowel. She wasn't even wearing any lipstick unless it was flesh coloured, his eyes hovering on her mouth. Turning his attention back to his coffee, he gave his head a shake before ripping off the plastic lid.

'There's sugar in the bag and a stirrer. I'll just start on this so it doesn't spill.'

'What about your sandwich?' she laughed, tilting her head up so, for the first time, their eyes actually met. Green like the cat he used to have as a child, now that was a shock. He continued to wonder if her hair would be blonde, brown, red or even pink.

'I'm not that much of a hard task master that you have to eat while you drive. What's your name by the way?'

'Oliver, and you?'

'Surely they would've told you that when they arranged the pick up?' A frown wrinkled her brow.

'It was too late by then. I'd just finished another job and was on my way…'

'Home, of course you were,' she laughed again but this time it was an unhappy sound. 'That's where everybody else is, home with their families and loved ones, and here we are, two strangers spending Christmas Eve together.' She shrugged away the thought, another smile on her lips. 'Call me Holly. I've never liked my surname and I certainly can't abide being called madam.'

She frowned again as he held out his hand and he realised his mistake because, of course, a real chauffeur wouldn't make such a gesture. Would a real chauffeur have plied his client with a drink when she'd expressly declined the offer? But it was too late now as she took hold of his fingers in the briefest of touches that sent a frisson of electricity up the back of his wrist and up under the sleeve of his grey worsted jacket.

'You're new, aren't you?'

'Yes mad— er—Holly. It's my first week.'

'That's what I thought,' her smile now teasing. 'Well, Oliver, you're doing fine, just fine but we probably should be...'

'Going?' his look blank.

'Yes, time is marching on. I'm sure you'd like to be back home to enjoy your day off tomorrow. I take it you are having a day off?'

'Yes.' He returned to his seat as if in a daze.

'Wife, family, kids?'

'What? No. I'm single. Never met the right woman,' he explained, indicating as he turned back on the M5 just past Bristol.

Now what had made him tell her that? There'd been plenty of women. In fact, there was one particular woman at the moment. Gerry seemed to be very keen to put their on-off relationship into the hands of the wedding planners. She'd even taken to leaving unsubtle hints about the benefit of a solitaire diamond over any other type of ring. If she'd had her way, he'd be on the Riviera even now, available to meet her every whim. It had only been his recent unavailability that had dampened her enthusiasm, but she was still there lingering in the background, the fear of course being that he'd weaken and say yes. He was well past the age when something in a short skirt and a low cut top turned him into a bowl of quivering jelly, despite all of her efforts.

His mind turned to the woman huddled under that cashmere coat. She could be wearing anything from jeans to a tutu but he very much doubted it. He sighed. He didn't even know her full name and yet he was able to gauge her taste in dress for heaven's sake. They were two strangers thrust together on a lonely snowfield stretch of road and in a little over two hours they'd never meet again. The sudden thought was as depressing as it was unnerving.

Chapter 5

What was the matter with her? She didn't normally chat to the paid help. She felt a flush trail across her cheek at the thought as she shifted in her seat. She hadn't been born a snob. In fact, her upbringing had been anything but. She really did appreciate the services of the people she paid to help her run her very busy life but calling them paid help was demeaning to both of them. It must have been when he shook her hand as the memory of his touch caused her breath to hitch. She'd never been a touchy-feely sort of person and, since the dissolution of her marriage, she couldn't remember the last time she'd allowed a man to get under her skin.

Staring down at her hands, she could still feel his fingers pressed into hers in a firm but gentle handshake. And then there was his eyes. She'd never seen eyes that particular shade of grey. She'd never known somebody could have grey eyes or were they just a light blue? No, they were grey; silver grey, maybe even stormy as her imagination got to work. Looking up, she glanced in the rear view mirror but all she could see was part of a cheek and the corner of a dark brow, which was probably a good thing. Men were more trouble than they were worth; twisting her wedding band round her finger as memories came flooding back.

She'd been happy to her wedding day, she'd never been happier. It seemed like fate had taken a hand in her falling in love with her would-be-stepbrother just when her father's time was drawing to a close. She couldn't remember her mother, which wasn't surprising as she'd been told she'd died when she was a baby and, for many years, there was just her and her father. He'd been both mum and dad to her and, being self-employed, she used to go everywhere with him. He had a small antiques shop on Wraysbury High Street and every Sunday they'd travel the country attending auctions and car boots looking for the affordable, unusual collectables he was famed for. It was on one of these trips he'd met Shirley and after what seemed like a whirlwind romance, two became four as Shirley had a son just a couple of years older than herself.

Everything had changed. In the beginning she hadn't even liked Kyle more than that and he certainly hadn't expressed any interest in a skinny, underdeveloped child. It was only later, just before her A-levels that he suddenly started picking her up from school on the back of his Harley Davidson. She was in love for the first time and instead of spending time with her father and Shirley, it was all about Kyle. She mouthed the name under her breath, squeezing her lids tight as the memories continued.

She was so wrapped up in this calf-love that she didn't realise until it was too late what was happening to her father. He was ill. He'd been ill for a while but suddenly the winter coughs and bouts of breathlessness put a stop to his weekly buying trips. She never completed her A-levels. She never even sat them. The morning she was meant to take her English she was sitting in the front pew of the church they'd never attended saying a final goodbye to her father.

She pushed away a rogue tear with an inpatient hand. Her father had been a good man, a kind man and she only hoped he'd known how much she'd loved him because it seemed to her that, now with the distance of time between them, she hadn't told him enough. It had only been the two of them until he'd met Shirley. All ifs and buts but too late to change a thing as a second tear followed on from the first. She'd been a fool, the biggest fool - Kyle had never loved her. He'd never even liked her and as for respecting her as a person...If she'd remained flat-chested he wouldn't have given her the time of day. But her bourgeoning body had finally kicked in with a vengeance when she'd turned seventeen, turning her from a tomboy into a teenage boy's page-three fantasy. She'd only learnt after the wedding about the bet he'd had with his best mate, Tony. She'd been on her way to change from her flowing, white gown into the pretty, pink dress she'd bought specially for her going-away outfit when she saw him huddled by the back door of the hotel counting a pile of notes. She'd been a bet, a miserly bet as to which one could bag the bird with the biggest bazookas.

She could have fled then but she didn't. Something, some self-preservation instinct made her thrust her chest out as far as it would go before grabbing him around the waist, her head nuzzling his back.

'Darling, I think there's time to be a little naughty before we have to leave,' she managed, throwing a wink at Tony. 'How about you grab some champers and come up in about fifteen minutes so I can slip into something sexy.'

She would have laughed at the way they were both staring at her, their jaws nearly hitting the floor, if she hadn't been struggling to hold back the tears. She'd managed, in the time allowed, to nip upstairs to their room before doing a flit down the fire escape with her passport and airline tickets.

'Everything alright in the back? We'll be turning off shortly.'

Glancing up, she saw his eyes reflected in the mirror and she knew he'd noticed the tears. Well, bully for him. She couldn't remember the last time she'd shed a tear. She wasn't an emotional person normally. No, that wasn't quite true. She wasn't an emotional person full stop. It must be the time of year, the snow and finally the meeting with Mr Pidgeon that had brought back a whole gamut of memories, some of them happy but most of them sad. But having some stranger look at her with concern radiating from his soft-grey eyes was only going to make her sadder.

'I'm fine, thank you, Oliver. How was your sandwich?' she managed, her voice sounding hoarse even to her ears.

'As good as can be expected. You didn't fancy yours then?' She looked at the wrapper lying untouched by her side. 'I wasn't hungry, after all. I think I'll get some shuteye,' she said, even as she wondered why she'd told him. He was paid to drive her, that was all and yet she was treating him as a new best friend, which was completely bizarre, in addition to being totally out of keeping with the way she normally treated men. Snuggling down under the rug in an effort to make herself more comfortable, she was surprised when he replied.

'Do you mind if I have the radio on. It'll help keep me alert.'

'No, that's fine.' Closing her eyes, she expected to hear some Christmas ditty instead she found herself listening to something that suspiciously sounded like Radio Three. A chauffeur with a taste for classical music was certainly a first in her book and one she was appreciative of. She'd have to get his full name before he left, and that was the last thought before sleep finally took hold.

'Bloody hell, that was close.'

She was dragged, kicking and screaming out of her dream; a dream where a mysterious stranger had kidnapped her and taken her to some isolated cottage. She was just getting to the good part where he was about to reveal his true identity when the sudden screech of tyres and then the curse wrenched her out of what was proving to be the best dream she'd had in years. She opened her eyes to the harsh reality of a white-filled winter wonderland.

'What's happened?' she croaked, leaning forward in her seat only to find her driver hunched over the steering wheel shaking like a leaf.

'Are you alright? Are you injured? Are you ill? What is it? Speak to me, Oliver?' her voice increasingly frantic when she got no response. She glanced out of the window again and then wished she hadn't. Where had the world gone? All around there was swirling snow slamming against the windscreen and nothing else.

She'd always loved snow as a child; her and her father, just the two of them, building a snowman out back and then the snowball fights, which he'd always let her win. They even went on sleigh rides using an old, tin tray he'd picked up somewhere or other. They were magical days followed by magical evenings warming chilled fingers in front of the open fire while roasting chestnuts and melting marshmallows. But this was different, different in a scary way - scarily different.

She shook her head in dismay at her thoughts, thoughts she hadn't allowed to surface for years. If she carried on like this she'd be an emotional wreck before she'd even reached the cottage. Heaving a sigh, she forced her attention back on the man in front.

'Oliver, tell me what's wrong and I'll help fix it,' her voice the one she used when dealing with her more supercilious clients. She was always firm but kind. She wouldn't be a pushover, not anymore.

'I—I shouldn't have agreed to this. It's madness.'

'Madness. Whatever do you mean?'

'Madam, Holly...' He removed his cap and laid it carefully on the dashboard before dragging one hand through his hair even as she noticed the other one curled around the gear stick, the knuckles bone white. 'Look, I'm not a chauffeur, alright. I don't even drive more than that and never in such bloody awful weather conditions.'

The silence within the car was deafening, matching the sudden silence outside as the wind dropped. It was as if they were cocooned alone in the world, just the two of them. The road was empty; empty both ahead and behind but she wasn't thinking about either the emptiness or the silence as she considered his words.

If he wasn't a chauffeur, just who the hell was he and, what had he been doing wearing a chauffeur's hat outside her apartment block? Was he a madman? She'd just been dreaming about being abducted. Maybe it wasn't a dream but a premonition? Had he kidnapped her? Was that what this was about? Was he going to demand a ransom for her release?

No, of course he wasn't. That was a stupid thought, as she eyed the back of his head. After all, she was the one who'd asked him to take her to the airport and then on to Cornwall. But if he wasn't a chauffeur then what was he?

Her eyes drifted back towards the window and any thoughts of interrogating him as to his intentions towards her stilled. It wasn't as if he was much of a danger in his present state and, to be quite frank, there were more important things to worry about at the moment than either her virtue or her bank balance. At this rate they were in danger of being stuck on a deserted road, in what looked like the middle of nowhere.

Undoing her belt, she wriggled through the gap between the seats before plonking herself in the passenger seat and adopting her 'dealing with a difficult client' voice.

'Now, Oliver, tell me what the matter is and where we are.'

'We're in the middle of nowhere, in the middle of a blizzard and I can't drive this car anymore,' his voice a hoarse croak.

'Okay, so we can't do anything about the weather. Do you know exactly where we are?' She watched him raise his head before tapping his finger on the satnav.

'I think we're here,' his finger pointing. 'Just coming up to the Tamar Bridge, if my memory serves me right.'

'What. You've been here before? You've been holding out on me, Oliver,' she said on a laugh. 'When we get back on the road I want to hear all about your exploits in sunny Cornwall. I can't believe you've driven so far, just how long was I asleep?'

'How am I meant to know? I had other things to think about,' his voice truculent.

'Of course, you did. Now, what we need to do is get back on the road as quickly as possible.'

'Are you mad as well as stupid? I've just nearly skidded into the bank and you want me to go out there again?'

She ignored his rudeness. He'd obviously lost it big time. If there was any way out of this mess, it was up to her to find it. She lowered her voice to a kinder, softer tone. 'Oliver, as far as I can see, we have two options. We can try and get to the cottage or we can stay here and freeze to death. I vote we opt for the cottage option myself.'

'Look, I'm sure you're a nice lady and all, but I don't think I can. It's so hard to see and, now the road surface is covered in white, I don't even know where the bank begins and ends. There's a good chance we'll end up in a ditch or, even worse, I could kill you.'

She heaved a sigh, her eyes taking in his trembling hands and grey-tinged skin. She'd thought him a man; a man's man. He certainly looked the part with his broad shoulders and tall frame. She'd thought him someone dependable, someone reliable; someone who wouldn't break under pressure. She'd thought him the kind of man who always knew what to do in any circumstance; someone who'd see it out whatever it was, and end triumphant. But she was wrong.

This was just a man, a man caught up in the most bizarre set of circumstances with, what was in effect, a stranger. She couldn't and she wouldn't expect anything from him.

'You're not going to kill anyone, Oliver. This is my fault. I've got us into this mess and I'll help get us out, but I can't do it alone. I asked you to drive me to Cornwall and, in hindsight, I shouldn't.' She pulled a face. 'It wasn't one of my cleverer ideas. In fact, it was bloody stupid. What you are going to do is start the engine and drive me to Polruan and I'm going to sit beside you and make sure you don't hit anything you shouldn't. Is that clear?'

He lifted his head and for the first time she realised what it was like to stare into someone else's soul. The anguish, the heartache and the pain were all there to see and she was the one looking. There was something more here. Something he wasn't telling her and something she couldn't begin to question. She wouldn't know what questions to ask. He looked haunted, at the end of his tether even. If she didn't play this carefully, they could very well end up dying on the side of the road somewhere near Cornwall. Changing her tone of voice as if speaking to a child, she touched his hand, trying to ignore the hairs along her arm standing to attention.

'We'll get through this, you and me. You're not alone, I'm here to help. I'll do whatever is necessary.'

She couldn't believe what she was about to do, so she didn't dwell on it. She just went with her instinct and, moving her hand from his arm to his neck raised her lips to his cheek before squeezing him in the tightest hug.

She'd kissed men before, of course she had but not many. Cheek kissing - French style - was in, after all, and she certainly wasn't interested in any other kind of kissing, French or otherwise. But those had just been brief pecks of skin meeting skin, before stepping away. This time she held him close, his head cradled in the crook of her neck just like she would a child. But this was no child. This was a man.

She shifted her fingers to the hair on the back of his neck not because she thought it would help soothe him but because she couldn't stop herself. He had thick, wavy, reddish-brown hair; hair that smelt of shampoo, her nose wrinkling. There was no fancy aftershave, or lingering cigarette smoke. There was soap and man, perhaps the deadliest of all combinations. She felt something shift, the cocoon she'd shrouded herself in splitting wide to reveal vulnerability and confusion.

She'd thought herself immune after all this time. Kyle had been eighteen years ago. Eighteen years since she'd been cradled by a man, not that he was doing much cradling, his hands lying limp by his sides. She'd had dates, boyfriends even but not one she would allow this close. At the first indication of more than a light touching of lips she'd backed off, and hence her reputation.

She didn't want to move and yet she did, her hand still on his arm, simply because she didn't want to let go of the feeling. There was strength here, just hidden under his grey, tailored jacket; strength and power. This wasn't a weak man as she'd thought. This wasn't a coward. This was an enigma. Something had happened to make him like this but she couldn't think about that now. Now they had to get out of this mess.

Her voice sounded strange to her ears, husky even and she wondered if he realised the emotions waging war under her breast. Here was a man, a different man; a man she wanted to cling to. She was a strong, independent woman who'd suddenly realised just what she'd been missing all these years. She used to be a cold-hearted, frigid bitch but not anymore.

'It will be alright. When we're sitting in front of that open fireplace, cracking open the bottle of champagne that's hidden in the bottom of my bag, we'll have a good old laugh about it. It will be something to tell your grandchildren in the future; that mad trip in the middle of a blizzard with some strange woman. They'll think you're a hero just like I think you're a hero to have gotten us this far with me snoring in the back.'

She grabbed the remaining sandwich simply for something to do with her hands other than touching him and, ripping open the plastic packaging, handed him one before taking a large bite out of the other and chewing reluctantly.

'We're going to spend two minutes eating this thing, sharing that water and then I'm going to get out of the car and clean the windscreen while you start the engine.'

'Has anyone ever told you how bossy you are?'

'No. Yes. You have, just now.' She smiled, relieved that he'd started to eat, the smile turning into a frown when he picked the window scraper from the dashboard. 'Now hold on a minute, where are you going?'

'If you think I'm going to let my passenger clean the windscreen, you have another thing coming. And I don't care how bossy...' he added, the rest of his words drowned by noise of the car door slamming behind him.

The windscreen was the easy part although she didn't know it at the time. He'd been gone at least five minutes and when he returned he was covered in fresh snowflakes.

'Brrr, its bloody freezing out there.' He rubbed his hands together, flexing his fingers under his gloves before starting the engine and putting the car into first. But instead of moving forward the only sound to be heard was the spinning of wheels as rubber met ice. The ice won.

'We're stuck, any bright ideas? I don't suppose you have a spade butting up to that champagne bottle by any chance?'

'Now that you mention it, no. I'm all out of spades,' her eyes searching the interior of the car. 'What's in the boot?'

'Your two bags. A food hamper with food in it. A toolbox with tools in it. No spade.'

'Mats.'

'Mats. Did you say mats?' he said, confusion stamped across his face. 'Is that some fancy new swear or something?'

'Car mats. Probably even better than a spade,' she said, trying to instil an optimistic tone to her voice and failing dismally. 'Come on and help. If we ram a car mat right in front of each tyre there may be enough grip for us to get back on the road.'

He stared at her for a second before grabbing her wrist and removing it from where she'd placed it on the door handle.

'Good idea, why didn't I think of that? But I'll do it. There's no point in both of us getting wet and cold.'

Chapter Six

It would've worked. It nearly worked. It did work, but not without disaster.

He'd placed the mats in front of each tyre just as she'd told him and then asked her to start the car while he pushed. It was a good idea. He'd lost his nerve for those few minutes but she'd talked him around. He couldn't tell her why he'd lost it. He didn't even want to think about it. Those dark days were best forgotten.

He was the strong one. He'd always been the strong one. He had one Achilles heel, just one, and that was snow because he knew of its dangers first-hand. He'd lost everything he'd ever loved in a Swiss avalanche. Snow was like the sea. It wasn't to be trusted. People didn't see the dangers. All they saw were snowmen and snowball fights, sleigh-rides and ski-slopes. He'd never been skiing since, despite the entreaties of his friends. They'd thought him lucky he'd escaped. But he hadn't escaped. His father had saved him by pushing him ahead before going back to help his wife. It was too late then. Once the snow had settled, he'd tried to dig them out, hands bleeding and frozen but he was too late. They'd survived but only long enough for him to say that final goodbye in the hospital.

He couldn't tell her any of that. She'd be upset, sympathetic even. She'd pity him and he'd seen more pity in the eyes of his friends and relatives to last him a lifetime. No, he'd get on with the job in hand. He'd start the blasted car, drive her to Cornwall and then…and then he'd have a rethink because he sure as hell wasn't prepared to spend too much longer driving around this hellhole.

'Right, go carefully. Put it into gear and ease off the brake. The one thing we don't want is you accelerating too fast.'

Hands in place on the bumper, he secured a strong foothold, the heels of his shoes driving through the snow and onto the tarmac.

'Right,' he shouted. 'Start the engine and slowly try and move it forward. On the count of three. One. Two. Three…'

He heard the car rumble to life, and then the faint vibration under his palms as she shifted the car into gear as he got ready to push. What he didn't expect was for her to slam down on the accelerator and shoot forward like a bullet out of a gun. What he didn't expect was to land flat on his face, his mouth, his nose suffocating with snow. He finally managed to twist himself onto his back, somehow aware that she'd stopped the car.

'Oh my God, are you alright?'

'Do I look alright? What the bloody hell do you think you were doing, woman?' his eyes wandering across the cloud-laden sky as he tried to regulate his breathing back to normal.

'I did what you asked.'

'No, you bloody didn't. What part of go easy on the accelerator did you not understand?'

'How dare you speak to me like that!'

'I dare, of course I dare. I'm the poor mug lying flat on his back with an injured…'

'Injured,' she interrupted, kneeling down beside him. 'You're injured? Where are you injured? Your back? Your leg? she said, starting to pat him down. 'Oh God, that's all we need. I can't drive.'

'You can't drive?' his voice incredulous. 'Why didn't you bloody well say so?'

'You didn't ask.'

'Oh, for heaven's sake.' He heaved a sigh before continuing. 'It doesn't really matter now, the damage is done,' he said, trying to stand up without putting any weight through his hand. 'I'm pretty sure it's only a sprain…I should be able to manage if you can help me back into the car? There's a *first aid box* in the boot if you could grab it?'

'And I've got paracetamol in my bag.'

'Well, we're sorted then, aren't we? All we need now is somebody to drive the car.'

He drove because he had to, he had no choice. She couldn't drive and there was no one else. His hand was throbbing and now almost twice the size but he still had his other one, in addition to both legs. The driving conditions were the worst he'd ever experienced but for now he could see out of the windscreen and by luck more than anything, Parker had decided that his next car would be an automatic. The one thing he'd lost completely was his sense of humour but he couldn't have everything.

True to her word, she hadn't returned to the backseat. She sat beside him to keep him company and it helped. Instead of thinking about the snow and the possible dangers ahead, they talked, if you could call it that.

'So, what kind of books do you enjoy reading?'

'I can't believe you've just asked me that.' He rolled his eyes. 'This isn't a date, Holly. This is two strangers stuck together in the most bizarre of circumstances and you're interested in what I read? You'll be asking me my favourite movies next. Ask me something useful, something interesting. Something you really want to know, not what I read or the music I listen to or how I like my tea. What about asking me what's the meaning of life? Something philosophical. Something deep.'

'That would be stupid,' she interrupted. 'And anyway, I know that already. It's forty-two.'

He smiled. 'Throw something at me. Anything, as long as it's not a date question. Something you'd ask one of your girlfriends?'

'Where did you buy that lipstick?' She giggled. 'Well, you did ask. Look, I'm crap at all this nonsense. I spend most of my day either trying to be nice to people I hate or trying to come up with ideas to improve an interior when, in most cases, it would be better leaving it alone. I'm far too old for small talk and dating was something I did in the last century.'

'Whoa, so much information there. To answer your question, I don't wear lipstick but, if I did, it would be that pale, pink shimmery kind like sugar frosting on one of those sickly sweet cakes.' His voice dropped a level as another memory popped out of nowhere and instead of snow, he saw his mother. She always came up the stairs to wish him a good night, whatever the time. And she always wore the exact same shade of lipstick. It must have been her favourite colour, he mused. Funnily enough it had always been his favourite colour, too. Not that anyone would ever ask a thirty-six-year-old bachelor what his favourite colour was. But if they did, he'd admit to red.

The image disappeared and, instead of his mother, he was confronted with the continued stretch of white in front of him and a conversation that needed resuscitating.

'What did you say you did again?'

'I didn't. I'm an interior designer.'

'Oh, something I'm bound to know a lot about them. So, what is it about your clients you so dislike? I take it it's your clients and not your work colleagues?'

'Where would you like me to start?'

'The beginning is usually a good place.'

'Well, there are two sorts of clients that usually darken my door. Those with new money and those from old,' she started, ticking them off on her fingers. 'Some have titles and goodness help you if you call them by the wrong one. But, whatever the size of their bank balance, they all have something in common – marital issues. They're either unhappily married, newly married and therefore so loved up as not to be taken seriously, or recently divorced.'

'Okay, can I ask a question?' he interrupted.

'You just have.'

'What do you have against marriage?' He took his eyes off the road for a second to throw her a glance because, for some reason, he really wanted to know. He'd always been clueless as to what went on in a woman's mind and, to be honest, he'd never bothered to delve too deeply because it wasn't their mind he was interested in. That is until just now. But when he saw the closed-down expression descend on her face, he knew he wasn't going to be any the wiser after this conversation; whatever answer she was planning it wasn't going to be the truth.

'I don't have anything against marriage. It's just the marriages I've seen have tended to be of the same sort.'

'But you're married?'

'So I am,' her tone closing the conversation just as if she'd slammed a door in his face. 'I take it you've been to this part of the world before as you recognised the Tamar Bridge?' she asked, changing the subject.

'Well, there was a signpost just before we came to it but yes, I have visited, but only the once,' his face wrinkling in a frown. 'I don't remember much, if I'm honest. I was with my father. My parents used to take a separate holiday at least once a year – something about keeping their marriage fresh or some such twaddle,' he said, flipping on the indicator before moving lane. 'I don't really remember. I was only about four...' Although that wasn't quite true as the sudden picture of his mother screaming at his father, tears streaming down her cheeks came out of nowhere. She hadn't wanted him to go and, after they'd returned, he was never allowed into their bedroom to share their bed for that early morning cuddle because his father had decamped into the dressing room.

Funny he'd only remembered that now after all these years. But memory was like that; a smell, a taste, a texture and he found himself free-falling backwards into the past to where he'd been happiest. Now, he wondered if he'd been the only happy one in their little family of three and if his parents had only been going through the motions for appearances sake?

'It sounds like they had a very modern marriage.'

'Does it?' His hand gripped the steering wheel. 'You might be right. I've been back a couple of times since, when I was at university but not to Polruan, to Fowey. The sailing, you know,' he added, veering the conversation onto more comfortable ground.

'Oh, University. What did you read?'

'Medicine.'

'And you ended up driving? Oh, no, you said you're not a chauffeur? I'd forgotten. So how come you agreed to drive me? What was that all about?'

'A fit of madness? Old age senility setting in a couple of decades early?' He gave her a wry smile even as he weighed up the pros and cons of telling her the truth. He never believed in lying, liars always got found out. He'd tell her as much of the truth as he was prepared to. There was no way he was going to tell her about his ancestry. Information like that was purely on a need-to-know basis.

'Ha, ha. You're not that much older than me.'

'How old are you then?'

She laughed. 'Did your mother never tell you not to ask a lady their age?'

'My mother is dead.'

'Oh, I'm sorry. I didn't mean to...I'm thirty-six,' the atmosphere going from friendly to awkward in an instant.

'There's no need for you to be sorry. It was a very long time ago, and I'm the same age.'

'Well, life begins at forty, or so I'm told.'

'That's good to know. There's a few years left for us both then. What date...?'

'June 5th,' she replied with a smile.

'Ha, you're older but I should have known with that bossy attitu...'

'Hey, I'm not bossy.' She raised an eyebrow. 'How much older?'

'Only a day, we're nearly twins, fancy that!'

'Yeah, fancy,' her voice dry. 'You were telling me why you agreed to drive me?'

'Persistent, aren't you, twinney? The cap belongs to my chauffeur, Parker. I was driving myself so he could get away early because...' he paused to glance at his watch. 'Because it was Christmas Eve. May I be the first to wish you a Happy Christmas, Holly,' he added with a chuckle. 'Not the kind of Christmas Day you were expecting, I'll bet.'

She shifted in her seat. 'Your chauffeur? What the hell made you agree to drive me to Cornwall then?'

'If you might remember, dear lady, I was only driving you to the airport?'

'But what about your own Christmas Day? Your family? Don't you have plans? How to make someone feel guilty in one fail swoop…'

He would have stopped the car if he hadn't been concerned that he wouldn't be able to start it again.

'There is no need to feel guilty. I was only planning a quiet day by myself. I like London best when there's nobody around. I would've probably taken a walk to Trafalgar Square to feed the birds, or perhaps strolled along the Thames to watch the boats.'

'Sounds a bit like the kind of Christmas I was planning before deciding to come down here.'

'Last-minute decision was it?'

'You could say that.'

'So, this house you're going to stay in? You haven't been there before? A new boyfriend?'

'No. It was bequeathed to me, yesterday in fact.' She smiled. 'Happy Christmas by the way. Not one you were expecting but hopefully there'll be some enjoyment somewhere.'

The landscape had changed considerably after passing over the Tamar Bridge. Now, instead of the long stretch of bleak motorway, there were small narrow lanes edged with large bushes and deep gulley's that the car struggled to avoid. The snow had stopped for now but the gloomy, yellow-grey light hovering like a dust cloud signalled that more was heading their way. There was no one about. The houses were few and far between. Stone cottages straddled the side of the road, the odd shadow thrown by an occasional Christmas tree, the only indication that they weren't the only people in the area - the only indication that it was Christmas.

Oliver stifled a yawn, rolling his shoulders back. He was stiff and tired and all he wanted was a nice hot bath and a warm drink, preferably with a heavy dollop of whiskey. But anything would do other than driving as his head started to ache in sympathy with his throbbing hand.

'We'll be there shortly. Polruan is only about ten minutes away. Do you have the address and I'll see what the satnav comes up with?'

'Forever cottage, Saint Saviours Hill. Apparently, it's right at the top.'

'Okeydokey.'

It took fifteen minutes in the end but five of those were spent trying to actually find the right road. It wasn't hard to miss the house, if you could call it that. It stood alone, at the end of a deserted track. A stark, stone-built building that looked more like a cowshed than any residence he'd ever stayed in. In fact, all that was missing was a mooing Daisy leaning her hairy head out of the window.

'Apparently this is it. Not much sign of life is there? How long has it been empty? It looks completely derelict,' his eyes drawn towards the white picket fence coated with a layer of snow.

She didn't say anything simply because she was as shocked as he was. Instead, she rooted in the bottom of her bag and pulled out an envelope, with a spidery crawl of letters on the side, before tipping the bunch of keys into her hand.

His forehead pulled into a frown, his eyes lingering on the words. The estate of Martha Branch, not the most common of names and yet it rang a bell somewhere inside his head as did the name of the solicitor stamped on the top being as it was the practice his father, and his father before him had always used. Martha Branch, an old-fashioned sounding name if ever there was one, and one he'd seen, on and off, most of his adult life.

Feeling her eyes swivel in his direction was all the impetus he needed to take the keys. He'd have to think about the implications of the name, but not now with the weight of her stare boring down on him.

'Careful, its slippery here,' his voice unsteady as he forced his attention off her face and onto her heeled boots. 'I hope you've brought other shoes with you,' he finally managed before opening the creaky gate and heading up the crazy-paving drive.

'And you call me bossy?' she huffed, as he fiddled with selecting the right key for the lock.

'If being a gentleman is bossy then call me bossy,' he replied, pushing the door open for her before flipping on the light switch.

The dull, low-watt bulb illuminated a small, square, white-washed room cluttered with heavy, mahogany furniture layered in dust. In fact, there was dust everywhere. Dust on the old, scarred wooden floor. Dust on the round, pedestal table and even in the fruit bowl but luckily no fruit. There was a wood-burning stove filling the stone mantelpiece and a large pile of kindling and logs so at least she would have heat.

Glancing out of the window with a frown, he suddenly realised there was no way he was prepared to leave her here. Shifting his gaze, he watched as she shook her coat, his eyes taking in her plain, black, cotton shirt and matching pencil skirt with interest. She had a good figure, a little too thin for his liking but with curves in all the right places and her hair... His gaze trailed upwards to watch as she removed her hat. He'd always been a sucker for long hair and hers flowed over her shoulders in a sleek salon waterfall of honey blond. He could drown himself in that hair as a sudden image of them naked, her hair brushing against his chest popped into his head and made it imperative for him to remove himself from her presence or embarrass himself forever. He'd guessed she was attractive, but not like this.

'I'll just bring the bags in,' he managed, pausing on the threshold, one hand on the old iron handle. 'Look, do you mind putting me up for the night? I don't think I can cope with...my hand. It's starting to throb.'

It was her turn to frown but her reply was all he could have wished. 'And I wouldn't expect you to. You're very welcome to share my supper and...'

A blush bloomed on her cheek as he hid a smile. She was happy to share her supper but not her bed. Well, what had he expected, for her to open her arms in grateful thanks? He'd sleep on the floor if need be. He just needed to sleep and not see that stretch of road again.

It took two journeys to-and-fro to bring in both of her bags and, at the last minute, he decided she might as well have his Fortnum and Mason's hamper too. After all, there was food enough to last her a couple of days.

Stamping his feet inside the door, he mirrored her actions with his coat before joining her in front of the wood-burner. She'd slipped off her boots and he hadn't realised just how petite she was, her head only reaching the top of his chest. Small but perfectly formed. The ache that had stopped him in his tracks only minutes before came back with renewed vengeance. He only hoped the cottage had a working shower because at this rate, he'd need it.

'How about I get this lit while you see about something to eat in addition to that champagne you promised?'

Chapter Seven

Polruan

Supper, by the warmth of the banked up wood-burner, was all she could have asked for, although she'd shrieked with laughter when she finally got around to setting the food out on the newly dusted table. She'd found plates, forks and glasses in one of the kitchen cupboards and, after a quick wipe with one of the tea towels hanging by the side of the sink, she'd started opening up packets and cutting bread. Staring at the large plate of salmon, it seemed that Oliver liked the same sort of food as her, even down to the type of bread and champagne. They'd even selected the exact same cheeses and brand of crackers to accompany them.

They had no tree. No baubles, no cards or any of the usual festive accoutrements but they were warm, well-fed and still had enough champagne to coat the sides of one last glass.

Oliver had pulled the sofa in front of the flames and, by mutual consent, they'd decided to eat off their laps.

'Coffee with that last glass? I didn't think to bring anything suitable for a nightcap.'

'Coffee would be lovely.' He leant back and stretched before getting up and helping her take the dishes into the kitchen.

'Leave them by the sink, Holly. I'll wash these up in the morning, there probably won't be enough hot water to do them tonight anyway and I don't mind if you don't?' he added, propping up the door jamb and watching as she filled the cafetière. 'While this is brewing, how about I investigate the bed situation, although, to be honest, I'd probably sleep standing up I'm so tired.

'You may very well have to,' she said quietly. 'I've already investigated and it's not good.'

He raised his eyebrows at the blush scoring her cheeks even as he thought how nice it was someone of her age still knew how. 'Not good as in no bed? No sheets? No blankets? What?'

'Well, there is a bed in the singular. Just one, and there is some bedlinen but not enough for the both of us.'

'Come on, show me,' he demanded, putting a gentle hand on her elbow. 'If you're going to force me to sleep on the floor at least show me what I'm missing.'

'Not much. I don't know what my mother was thinking,' her voice soft as she walked through the lounge and into the small hall. 'There's scarcely room to swing a cat let alone sleep one,' she added, pushing the door open on a room little more than the size of a cupboard. All the floor space was taken up with either a small double or large single, he couldn't quite make up his mind at the moment, his eyes lingering on the single pillow and a couple of thin blankets.

'It's yours, of course. You did all the driving and your hand...'

'My hand's fine and there is no way I'm going to take the bed when you sleep on the...'

'Couch. I'm sleeping on the couch, Oliver, and that's final. I'm only short so I'll easily fit. I'll be as warm as toast in front of the stove with my coat and the car rug, if you'll let me borrow it?'

'Of course,' his look intense. 'I take it there's no way you'd agree to share? After all, there's not much to you and I'm not exactly fat. It would be much warmer and I promise I'll behave. I'm too tired to be amorous.'

'You're right. There's no way I'd agree to share. It's the bed, or the floor, doctor. The choice is entirely yours.'

It wasn't the cold that kept her from settling, although her feet did feel like a couple of ham hocks left behind in the bottom of the freezer. It wasn't the size of the couch, which was just that little bit too small, just as it wasn't the sound of the wind howling down the chimney forcing plumes of smoke and sparks from the stove. It was the memories. Her memories of Kyle, who was someone she hadn't thought of in such a long time.

She hadn't heard from him since that fateful day outside her solicitor's office when the annulment had finally come through after the longest eight months of her life. He'd sworn then she owed him big time and, in truth, she still believed that he'd get his own back some day when she was least expecting it. It didn't matter that he'd already got himself a new girlfriend by then and was building up a reputation as a buy-to-let entrepreneur. She'd made him a laughing stock in front of *his bestie* and for that she'd pay. It had taken her a long time to stop looking over her shoulder but, moving to London and then reverting to her mother's maiden-name made it less likely that he'd find her.

'Can't you sleep either?'

The sound of his voice from the end of the sofa nearly had her leaping two feet in the air but it was the sight of him padding around bare-foot and bare-chested that really did the damage.

Who knew he'd been hiding *that* under his conservative grey two-piece, her eyes lingering seconds longer than they should on his broad shoulders before dipping down to his red boxers and back up again? What was that word again she'd overheard on the tube last week? Ripped, that was it. If anyone deserved that label it was him.

Her thoughts, so recently on Kyle flickered backwards but there was little to compare. Kyle had been puny and yet with the makings of a paunch and a double chin, whereas Oliver didn't have an ounce of spare flesh or a trace of fat. Here was a man who clearly looked after himself both in diet and fitness as her heart started tap-dancing against her chest wall. Here was a man whom she was staring at with her jaw reaching her knees, another blush screaming across her cheeks as she forced herself to look towards the window.

'Er, no,' she finally managed, her heart spluttering to a complete halt at the feel of his hand on top of her foot.

The shiver coursing up her leg as skin met skin caused a frown to pierce his brow. He obviously thought she was cold and she wasn't about to put him right. How could she tell him that her temperature had just sky rocketed through the roof, any additional heat source and she might very well internally combust.

'God, you're freezing. I'm not surprised. The fire's gone out.'

'I'm fine, really.'

'Really?' his eyes boring into her. 'I think not. Look, I'll put the kettle on and make us a hot drink while you go and hog the bed. I have no intention of dealing with a case of double pneumonia.'

'I—I can't,' her voice tumbling into a stutter.

'Yes you can. I won't tell your husband, if you won't and, as I've already told you, I'm too tired to be amorous so no launching yourself on my weak, male body or I might just throw up.'

'Charming,' but she managed a laugh of sorts, slipping her arms into the sleeves of her coat before standing up. He wasn't the type to poach on another man's property, not that she was any man's property but he wasn't to know that. That part was best left forgotten.

Placing her coat across the end of the bed for their feet she glanced down at her pyjama-covered body. He'd have to be desperate to try, kitted out as she was in top to toe flannelette with all of the buttons firmly closed up to her throat. Propping herself up in bed she planted what she hoped was a smile on her lips at the sound of him stomping down the hall.

'Hot milk,' he said, throwing her a quick glance. 'How old did you say you were, again? You look about twelve in those plaits.' He sat down on the side of the bed before slipping his legs under the sheet.

'You just go on thinking I'm twelve and we'll get along just fine,' her hand cradling her cup with interlaced fingers as she took a cautious sip. 'Just what the doctor ordered, by the way.'

'My pleasure, madam,' his voice slightly hoarse as he switched off the bedside light and rolled onto his side. 'Sleep well.'

Funnily enough that's what she did. Following his example, she turned onto her side and was soon in a deep, dreamless sleep where nothing would have woken her.

The snow carried on muffling and insulating the building, blowing its white fury into every nook and crevice. The car wasn't immune to its charms as it dripped and spread itself over Parker's pride and joy with no thought for the highly polished paintwork. It was as if it took pleasure in obscuring everything in its wake, cocooning the two strangers in their white prison before dipping and dying into the dark glow of Christmas morning. But still this pair of mismatched travellers slept on, ignorant of what lay outside. Ignorant of the distant church bells heralding this special day.

It was the silence that woke her, the silence only interrupted by the slight snore coming somewhere into her neck. Lying still, she controlled and finally conquered the sudden fear as memories of yesterday surfaced.

He wasn't a threat, this Oliver, far from it as her eyes swivelled to take in the way his leg, during sleep had trapped her to the mattress like some erstwhile lover. But still he slept on, only muttering a slight groan of protest as she eased away and escaped from under his weight. She stood then, examining him as if for the first time. In truth, the first time she'd been alone in a bedroom with a man that wasn't her father.

He looked younger somehow. His frown and laughter lines smoothed out, his mouth soft instead of firm, the little cleft in his chin now darkened with morning stubble. She felt something shift inside at the sight of that shadowing along his jaw, her hand flexing in an effort to control the sudden need to rasp her fingers along his skin.

Desire was an ugly word, or at least ugly to someone like her. Someone that had suppressed all hope, all need, all of her private yearnings for affection and love. No, she hadn't suppressed them. She'd stamped on them, smashing them to smithereens, or at least she'd thought she had but now... But now she wasn't so sure. He was a good-looking man, this Oliver, her eyes now on his bare chest where the blanket had shifted down to his waist. He was a good-looking, powerful man.

She paused, her hand drifting to her throat at where her thoughts were leading her. What if he'd woken first? What if he'd crawled out of bed without disturbing her only to pause on the threshold to examine her curves and lines? What would his thoughts have been? He'd thought her skinny, she remembered as her mind pulled her to last night and her full plate. He hadn't made an issue of it but she sensed his disapproval at the uneaten meal. How could she tell him that ever since Kyle and his comments, food had been an anathema? She wasn't anorexic, far from it and she certainly wasn't bulimic but she did assess each forkful before it passed her lips. Eating now wasn't a pleasure but a chore. She ate to survive, no more, no less.

She walked across the room only to pause and then return to the bed. He'd turned in his sleep, his arms now cuddling the pillow to his chest, the blanket riding dangerously low on his hips. With a careful hand she lifted the cover and draped it across his shoulder. She wanted to do more, so much more but she didn't. Instead, she escaped into the comfort of the shower, locking the door securely behind her.

Later found her in the kitchen humming a gentle tune. She'd dressed in black jeans and t-shirt, before pulling on her favourite black polo-neck lambs-wool jumper. Her hair she'd dragged into a messy bun before starting the first of her morning chores.

She employed a 'woman that did' in London simply because she could spend longer in the office. Mrs Fitzgerald, a widowed cockney, was as much a nuisance as a joy simply because of the chatter that accompanied each waking breath. She knew her life story within five minutes of meeting, and each visit was an excuse for an update on her extended family. EastEnders had nothing on the escapades of her daughter, Sharon. What with her two husbands, both of which had served time, not to mention her six kids, all from different fathers - each visit had her glued to the sofa with a mug of tea as thick as syrup as she waited for the next instalment.

She'd never found domestic duties fun. Housework bored her senseless but now... now she was enjoying herself. No, she wasn't *just* enjoying it - it was fun. Who knew?

She'd pulled back the dull, brown curtains and had to suppress the laugh, building in her throat, at the sight of Oliver's car cloaked in a thick blanket of snow. There was no way he was going anywhere today, even as she frowned at the sudden infusion of delight that seemed to take her breath away. It was only because she didn't want to be alone, she reasoned. After all, she was in a strange part of the world, at least strange to her, and the company of a powerful man like Oliver was comforting. Shaking her head with annoyance, she made short work of cleaning the stove and setting a new fire before heading to the cupboard off the hall in search of a dustpan and brush.

She laughed then. She laughed out loud at the sight which greeted her. Instead of the mop handles, brooms and dusters she'd been expecting, she found a flight of stairs; a flight of stairs that led to the most amazing double bedroom, complete with king-sized bed and matching mammoth duvet.

She nearly threw herself into the middle, rolling the duvet around her in a massive cocoon but she didn't. Instead, she walked towards the window to stare in amazement at the panoramic view below. The cottage was on the top of a hill overlooking Fowey estuary and, presumably, the Cornish village of Fowey now sugar-coated with snow. Reaching out a hand, it was almost as if she could curl her fingers around the tiny cottages pinned back against the hill opposite.

Instead of staring at the view, a view she could never tire of, she traipsed back down the stairs and into the kitchen to explore. It was past breakfast time, something she didn't need the hands of a clock to remind her as her stomach moaned its annoyance. It was breakfast but she hadn't thought to throw any cereal into her bag, and Oliver's Fortnum and Mason's hamper added little to the mix, apart from a jar of homemade strawberry jam. Perfect, except they'd finished the last of the bread.

Opening all the cupboards was like entering Aladdin's cave. Her mother had obviously been something of a hoarder and, as the daughter of an antiques' aficionado, Holly thoroughly approved. She could have spent hours examining the plates, bowls and dishes stacked in the pine cabinets but right now, food was more important than crockery. For a reason she wasn't prepared to examine too closely, she wanted to present Oliver with a breakfast he'd appreciate. There was flour and yeast stacked away in the larder cupboard and she immediately set some oats to soak before flinging handfuls of flour into one of the heavy earthenware bowls.

It had been a long time since she'd made bread, years even but lessons learnt at the hands of her home-economics teacher came flying back as she activated the yeast into a bubbling frothy mass before adding it to the flour and kneading as if her life depended on the outcome of her ministrations. Setting it aside to prove, she fiddled with the stove before finding a pot for the porridge and soon the kitchen smelt like a kitchen again with fresh coffee in the percolator and bread rising in the oven.

Sitting at the table with her second coffee of the day, she was just wondering whether she should wake him when she heard a noise behind her.

Chapter Eight

Ollie stood in the doorway tucking the tails of his less than pristine white shirt into the waistband of his trousers.

He hated not having clean clothes. In fact, he couldn't remember the last time he'd had to don anything other than a freshly washed, not to mention freshly ironed, shirt. His housekeeper, Mrs Grant, was a marvel. She even ironed his boxers, not that he asked her to or anything. All he did at the end of each day was strip off his clothes into the laundry basket inside his bathroom and hey presto, as if by magic, every morning he found his walk-in wardrobe replenished with a fresh supply.

His student days were the nearest to hell he'd ever come what with having to organise his own washing at the local laundrette. But an ironing board was as foreign as a steam iron and, as a young man he'd made do with t-shirts and jeans. But now he had an image to maintain.

He wasn't vain unless the need for good hygiene could in any way fall under that banner. No, he was fussy as opposed to being a fusspot; meticulous as opposed to finicky. Perhaps if things continued on their current course there was a threat that his liking of things his own way would end in an overbearing fastidiousness but, for now, he just hated the feel of day-old clothing against his skin.

'You should have woken me,' he said, moving towards her.

'Why? It's Christmas Day, surely not a day for clock watching—?'

'All the same...' he eyed her warily, taking in her black garb with a frown. What was it with all this black anyway? She was obviously a very attractive woman with the most delightful curves, he mused, his gaze wandering fleetingly to her chest, and yet she dressed as though she wanted to disappear, to turn invisible. He just didn't get it but, as her driver, it wasn't really his business. He'd have something to eat and then make tracks as he forced a smile on his lips. The thought of spending the rest of Christmas holed up in some impersonal hotel, something that yesterday had seemed idyllic, now left him cold. He'd just head back to London and see if his steak was still edible...

'How's your wrist,' her voice interrupting his thoughts like a lifeline.

'Oh, fine. Much better.' He wandered across to the coffee maker and lifted up the jug. 'Would you like a top-up?'

'Please,' she smiled. 'I'm afraid we've run out of milk though.'

'That's fine. I take mine as it comes; a remnant of student days when someone always used up the last of the milk.'

'Talking of student days...I'm afraid breakfast isn't going to be a *full-English*. You do have a choice, though,' she added, her eyes twinkling.

'Well, a choice is always better than no choice.'

'Yes, there's porridge with salt, or there's porridge with sugar?'

'Ah, with salt then, thank you,' his smile mirroring hers. 'Have you eaten or may I keep you company?'

'No, I was waiting until...' She started to stand, only to pause at the weight of his hand on her shoulder.

'No, let me serve you. After all, you were the one that let me sleep on.' He still couldn't quite believe he'd managed to sleep without the whiskey crux he'd been beginning to rely on, not that he was complaining or anything. Life, which yesterday had been a disaster zone, a chore even, now held a wealth of possibilities and all because of a good night's sleep. Tonight he'd be back in his own bed with its feather mattress and down duvet and, with a bit of luck, he'd sleep right through Boxing Day and beyond, as thoughts of London reminded him of his pending trip.

'I'll make tracks after. I might be able to make the motorway before darkness,' his voice resigned as he stepped towards the bubbling pot on the stove and started ladling out large bowlfuls.

'I think not.'

'Pardon?'

He placed a bowl in front of her before sitting down, all his attention now on the quiet girl opposite. No, that wasn't quite right. She wasn't a girl, even though she'd scraped back her hair somehow or other. He wasn't an expert on hair or indeed on any part of a woman's apparel but the messy hairstyle that framed her face with soft tendrils was lovely; lovely but deceiving as it took years off her age. This wasn't some young girl. This was someone with both the mind and body of a woman, something he'd found out last night when she'd snuggled next to him. It had taken all his self-control not to reach out a hand to investigate those womanly curves that were pressing up against him through the innocence of sleep. Instead, he'd rolled her onto her side, anchoring her in place with his knee flexed into her back while he tried to switch off all senses. What happened after that wasn't his fault as a flush scored his cheeks.

'I said, I think not. Have you happened to look out of the window this morning? It must have snowed pretty much all night.'

'As long as I can get to my car...'

'You won't be able to even see it. It's disappeared under a snow drift.'

'Really?' his voice incredulous. 'Surely not?'

'Well, if you don't believe me...Have your porridge while it's hot and then I'll show you,' she said, lifting her spoon and starting to eat. 'There's bread too, or there will be in a few minutes.'

'I thought we'd finished it last night?'

'I made a couple of loaves this morning.'

His eyes widened. 'Quite the little homemaker.'

'It was that or starve, although the freezer does appear to be full. It won't be fresh but at least I'll be able to produce something edible.'

He rested his spoon down in his empty bowl. 'If your porridge is any indication of your cooking abilities, it will be more than edible. That was delicious.' He stood up and, picking up the empty dishes, proceeded to fill the sink with water

'There's no need to...'

'It's only fair as you did the cooking.'

48

'But your hand—?'

'My hand is pretty much back to normal,' as he held out both for her inspection. 'See, no sign of redness, inflammation or swelling,' he said, noting the absence of tremor with a frown. He'd been off sick now for three months, three months in which to regain the nerve he'd lost on that faithful day. He was lucky to be able to control a spoon let alone a scalpel. But now, after just one night of blissful sleep, things appeared to be on the mend. He couldn't believe how much his life had changed since, or the sense of relief that finally he might be over the worst. His one worry, of course, was that it wasn't just time that had initiated his recovery; time and the stress and upheaval of the journey having somehow shocked him into healing. His gaze flickered towards her. He was scared that his attraction for this woman had played a part and time would only tell if he was right.

'And anyway,' he managed, his eyes clashing with hers even as he admired the clear, emerald green of her gaze. 'Surely you can't want some strange bloke invading your personal space not to mention sharing your only bed?'

'Er—about that...'

'Yes,' his senses now on full alert.

'Yes, well there are more bedrooms as I discovered this morning so there was no reason for us to...'

He hadn't realised she was the kind of woman to feel embarrassed as he watched the way her fingers twisted round and round her mug. He'd thought her one of those modern, independent women in charge of their own destiny. Raising his own mug, he suddenly wondered what else she was going to prove him wrong about as he remembered the lovely creamy porridge and the smell of homemade bread gently browning in the oven. He'd made assumptions yesterday, assumptions she was tearing down one by one. He'd thought her a product of the refined London society he avoided like a traffic jam. How wrong could he be as he noticed she'd barely combed her hair not to mention the complete absence of make-up, and as for her clothes. Her outfit couldn't be termed as anything other than functional even if what it hid met with his approval. She was still too thin but with a few extra pounds she could very well be his ideal woman. Clearing his throat, he tried to remember that sliver of gold on her finger. If he'd been her husband, he certainly wouldn't have taken kindly to her going off gallivanting, Christmas or no Christmas.

'Ah and here I was thinking you enjoyed snuggling up next to me,' he teased, enjoying the deepening bloom on her cheeks.

'Hardly. Come on, I'll take you on a guided tour.'

They stood, side by side, peering out of the bedroom window and across the estuary. It was a fine crisp day now, without a hint of snow in the air, which made a mockery of the deep snowdrifts littering the driveway and gardens stretched out before them.

'See, there's your car,' she pointed. 'Just in front of that tree.'

'That's a tree? Are you sure?' He groaned, realising just how isolated and snowed-in they actually were. But it was Christmas Day; he could probably afford to hang around until tomorrow. In fact, he couldn't leave her all by herself in such circumstances. What if the fire went out or the lights failed? Or, unlikely as it was, what if a stranger came along—?

'I'm sorry; it seems I'm going to have to impose on your hospitality for another night,' as he noticed her face tighten into a frown.

For someone like him, with the self-esteem of a potato, the sight of her annoyance was just one more stab in the back as his heart lurched towards his socks. She thought him an irritant, probably like everyone else across the Southern Hemisphere even as his wicked gene kicked in. If she was annoyed now, he might as well see how far he could push it. He might as well do what he'd wanted to ever since she'd first called him Oliver even as he wondered if he'd be sleeping in the shed tonight.

'So, what are we going to do for the rest of the afternoon, then?' his eyes flickering briefly to the bed and back to her face.

He knew what he'd like to do but how to broach the subject…? In his present state of confusion, it would be impossible to ask, but perhaps he could show her.

50

He eased his arm over her shoulder, his eyes shifting, burning a trail and suddenly the tempo of the conversation slowed as speech met desire head-on and desire won. His mouth lowered, as if of its own accord, his lips brushing against hers in that first kiss.

As first kisses went, it wasn't anything to write home about and it certainly didn't give any indication of what was to come. In fact, it could be anyone he was kissing; a friend, a relative, a colleague, but it wasn't. There was also no indication of the explosion of senses that punctuated the air in wave after wave of passion. Suddenly there was no Holly and no Oliver. There was no lord and commoner. There was no surgeon and interior designer. There was no past, present or even future. There was a man and a woman, feeling their way blind along the gamut of emotions washing over them in a tide of unprecedented desire. Mouths opened, pressure increased and tongues started that intimate game that only lovers know the rules to. But there were no rules. The kiss was endless and yet seemed to stop all too soon for both of them. Eyes held; passion dimmed and confusion, topped with a large dollop of embarrassment, kicked in.

'I'm sorry; I didn't expect that to happen,' he whispered, his forehead resting against hers as he struggled to regain his equilibrium.

'Neither did I and especially not after…' she managed, her smile a little dazed.

'After?'

'Nothing.'

She refused to meet his eyes and he knew he'd blown it. He'd have the kiss to remember but that was all. It was as if they were strangers again, meeting for the first time, although strangers with heavily bruised lips and awkward smiles.

Chapter Nine

God, what was wrong with her all of a sudden? She tried and failed to prevent all sorts of naughty thoughts from coming into her head after that kiss. He wouldn't be interested in a woman like her, not unless he was desperate, and sex wasn't something she'd ever take lightly. In truth, it was something she'd never taken. It was always there on the horizon as something other people did, something messy and emotional that a cold-hearted bitch like her was unable to enjoy or respond to. Her last relationship, if two dates could be called a relationship, had ended in disaster when he'd taken the goodnight kiss as an excuse to maul her with his marauding hands and plundering lips. She'd ended up pushing him away with such force that he'd crashed against the wall, but she hadn't cared. All she'd cared about was making it into the safety of her apartment and bolting the lock on his nasty words shouted through the letter box.

And yet now all she could think about was the weight of this man's leg as it had pinned her to the mattress and the feel of his bristly chin against her skin. He still hadn't shaved and the dark shadowing only went to aid and abet the image of dominant male, an image she was pretty sure he wasn't aware of. Her hormones were in overdrive and her common sense was mush at her feet. She wanted this man's babies – what a thought.

She cleared her throat with a nervous cough as her eyes looked anywhere but at him. 'I thought I'd have a look around and start clearing some stuff out. You can help if you like?'

She walked over to the built-in wardrobe and, yanking back the door, unveiled hanger upon hanger of evening dresses. 'I remember my father telling me my mother had a thing for vintage clothes, one of the only times he'd talked about her...' her fingers trailing through the brightly coloured fabrics. 'If old clothes aren't your thing there's also a TV in the lounge if you just want to hole up with whatever blockbuster is on?'

'Hardly, I doubt we even have reception.'

'Oh, I didn't think to check…'

'What, your husband hasn't phoned to wish you a Happy Christmas?' he raised his eyebrows.

'I'm divorced. And you? No wife, girlfriend, significant other…?'

'Nope, only me,' his eyes on her hand where it hovered over a long, flowing, pale pink gown. 'That's pretty. You still wear your ring?'

'It's very useful in controlling male urges,' she said, placing the dress to one side before continuing her rummaging.

'Is that what they're called? I'll have to remember in future. So men, strange men, do they often pester you with their— er—male urges?'

'A certain type, usually the married ones. I'm not very big or particularly strong but I don't need to be if they think I've got a man behind me.'

'What! Do they—?' his voice sharp.

'Rarely.' She threw him a quick smile over her shoulder.' I'm getting on a bit now. There's always someone prettier, younger and certainly more willing to accept their attentions so I get let off the hook.'

'Thank God. Although they have it wrong, of course.'

'Wrong? I'm confused,' her look wary as she added a stunning yellow gown with balloon sleeves to the pile.

'There's no need to be,' he said, touching the silky gold fabric with his fingertips. 'Women are like wine. They only get better with age.'

'So now I'm Methuselah, great! Look, there's no need to flatter me just because I'm putting you up for the night. I only have to look in the mirror to see the truth staring back at me.'

'It must be a very funny mirror. Or perhaps it's the woman looking into it that's the problem?'

She felt his eyes wander up and down and now her whole body blushed, but not with embarrassment.

'How dare you look at me like I'm something on a slab for sale to the highest bidder - and you a doctor too? I thought with that Hippocratic Oath you'd be above all that?'

'All what? I might be a doctor but I'm also a man; a gentleman,' his voice deceptively soft and she knew she'd angered him. But his feelings, whatever they were, weren't going to stop her. She'd thought him different. He wasn't – he was just like all the rest.

'If you were a gentleman you wouldn't speak to me like that,' her eyes flashing. 'So what sort of a doctor are you anyway? A surgeon? A cardiologist? A psychiatrist? A gynaecol…?'

'I'm a plastic surgeon.'

She felt her mouth open and close like a fish but no words came out and he obviously wasn't going to help her out of the ruddy great hole she'd just dug for herself.

'Well, that's just great. That's all I bloody need. What do you think that's going to do for my self-confidence now? Why couldn't you be something normal like a GP?' She edged towards the bed and sat down simply because her legs wouldn't hold her up for a second longer. He was still looking at her but now instead of frowning there was a look of concern.

'Because I'm not, and what has me being a plastic surgeon got to do with how you look?'

'I hate the way I look, alright. I hate every little bit of me, but most of all I…' her throat suddenly awash with tears.

'You what, Holly? Although that's the wrong question, isn't it? It's not what you hate about how you look. It's why?'

He didn't come to her like she half expected. He maintained his distance just as he maintained his iron control on the conversation. It was her that was breaking down into a complete mess.

'From where I'm standing I see a very beautiful woman,' he continued. 'I know lots of women who'd kill and more to look as good as you do and yet here you are hiding away in widow's weeds. The only problem is your weight.'

'What, I'm fat? Oh great, I hardly eat as it is and now you're calling me fat.'

'Hardly, you're thin, too thin. If you were my wife, I'd take pleasure in filling you with chocolates and cakes to pad out all those curves that are begging for nourishment.'

'Well, you're not and I'll thank you to keep your opinions to yourself for the length of time we have to be stuck together,' her eyes now firmly rooted on the window.

'The cottage is large enough for you not to be bothered by my company,' his only reply as he stormed out of the room, banging the door closed behind him.

She sank back against the mattress, like a rag doll with all the stuffing knocked out of her, even as hot tears tracked down her face. Of all the people to be marooned with she had to choose a bloody plastic surgeon, a man expert in the beauty of others, as she allowed her emotions free reign. He'd said she was beautiful, if a little thin but what did he know, and yet why would he say it? Surely there was no need to butter her up? It wasn't as if she was going to kick him out into the snow no matter what her thoughts on the matter. He obviously viewed people, women as something to improve so why wasn't he seeking to make some money?

She placed her hands on her breasts, something she usually avoided at all costs. She just about managed to examine them as she was meant to for those monthly checks but that was all. She washed them; she housed them in the most basic of cotton coverings and tried to forget about them. She only ever wore black, her wardrobe only contained black. Nothing low-cut or too-tight. Nothing revealing. Nothing to emphasise or accentuate. She'd bind them if she didn't think it might not harm them and yes, she'd even considered having plastic surgery. Part of her knew it was madness. There were women out there with a lot more on offer and still they wanted more but, for her, the weight of Kyle's ugly comments outside her solicitor's office had done the everlasting damage they were meant to.

She woke up with a start, unable to fix on where she was or what she was doing lying in bed. The curtains were pulled closed where before they'd been open just as the rug on the bottom of the bed was now pulled up to her shoulders.

There could only be one explanation. He'd come and checked on her after her little outburst. She remembered her words and what she'd accused him of. She'd insulted his profession and she'd insulted him as a man but she'd been hurt. He'd hurt her with his words. What gave him the right to question her like that? He had no right.

She struggled to sitting and, swinging her legs over the side, looked around for her slippers but she didn't have to look far. He must have placed them beside the bed just where she could reach them. But then again, as a doctor, he'd know about such things. Brushing her hair off her face, she noticed her hairclip beside her on the pillow and realised he'd done more than remove her slippers. He'd made sure she was both warm and comfortable, but that was all.

She must have been more tired than she'd thought as she saw the bedside clock heading towards five pm. What a great Christmas this was turning out to be.

'Ah, you're awake. Talk about being out for the count...' He stood just inside the doorway, but instead of saying anything about their altercation it was as if it had never happened. Instead of words, he headed for the bedside table with a mug, making sure she could reach it before finally speaking.

'Dinner's nearly ready but I thought you might like a coffee. Falling asleep during the day can be a little unsettling.'

She met his gaze. 'I'm sorry about earlier, I'd like to apologise for insinuating...'

'Think nothing of it and it was my fault. I shouldn't have interfered. After all, we are ships that pass in the night, nothing more. Your body, your life, your business.' He smiled down at her. 'Come down when you're ready. I'm no chef but hopefully it will taste good.'

'So, did you have to use every dish in the house?' her laughter ringing out across the kitchen at the sight of the piled-up sink. 'I take it I'm doing the washing-up then?'

'No, we'll share it,' his grin rueful, as he raked his hand through his hair. 'My housekeeper rarely lets me in the kitchen.'

'I'm not surprised,' although she lessened the impact of her words with a smile. 'Something smells amazing. I was worried we'd be having baked beans on toast.'

'Yes, well we may very well have to resort to that dietary staple but I do hope not. There's garlic bread to start and I found a chicken down the bottom of the freezer, so roast chicken with stuffing, roast potatoes (Aunty Bessie's best) and sprouts,' he ended with a grimace. 'I can't abide them but it was the only frozen veg in the freezer and they are sort of traditional aren't they? I've spiced them up a bit though – I hope you like chilli?'

'I love it. So, what can I do to help? Plates? Set the table?'

'All sorted. I even found the drinks cabinet so, what about an aperitif?' He cleared his throat before continuing. 'I wasn't snooping, just trying to find something alcoholic, but I came across a box of photos. I left them on the sofa...'

Dinner was forgotten, or at least for her. She noticed the soft, candlelit table with its shining cutlery but all of her attention was taken up with the shoebox he'd found. She didn't even notice when he set a martini down in front of her, intent as she was on removing the lid on her mother's memories.

Funny the way the word *mother* traipsed across her mind, a word she hadn't thought of in years; mother, mum, but never mummy. Not that she could remember her. How could she when she'd been led to believe she was dead? She'd been ten when her father had started dating Shirley; Shirley, the closest she'd ever come to having that sort of a mother/daughter relationship and just look how that had turned out. She'd been eleven when Shirley had moved in as his live-in business partner/lover and after that she'd been too tied up with a new school, a new life, a crush on her would-be-step-brother that she'd forgotten to even ask about her mother. She'd forgotten until Mr Pidgeon had reminded her.

He'd been looking for her for weeks, ever since her mother had been taken unwell and then died so unexpectedly. He'd even been in touch with Kyle but he'd professed to have no idea as to her whereabouts. He didn't comment then on how rude he'd been but she could guess by his barely concealed frown. He'd only found her by luck when Lady Nettlebridge's daughter, Titania Brayley, had popped in to ask him whether he'd like to be Godfather to her firstborn. One thing had led to another and, when they got to discussing Lady Nettlebridge's charity endeavours and the new ballroom she was having commissioned by Holly Branch Interiors, the rest fell into place.

Her fingers hovered over the top photo; a photo of her as a teenager and everything suddenly made sense. Her father must have maintained contact despite Shirley, and despite letting her believe her mother had died all those years ago.

It was the last photo taken of her with her father, a day stolen from all the others. It had been her birthday, her seventeenth and Shirley and Kyle had decided to get up early to attend a car boot at Charnock Richard's.

Staring at the curled edges, she remembered she'd been upset that they hadn't invited her, that Kyle would rather spend the day with his overbearing mother than with her but then her father had made everything better; he'd hired a car and they'd spent the most delicious day doing all the things they wanted to but never seemed to have the time. They'd popped into the local library first and spent a quiet hour choosing a pile of books before heading for the River Thames with a picnic to die for. They'd laughed, remembered, cried a little and then toasted with her first taste of champagne before curling up on the grass and flicking through their books. He'd given her a cheque, she remembered. Money to fritter away on whatever she wanted and she'd bought that tight-fitting blouse in the window of the dress shop just around the corner. It had been pink with the most delightful lace-edged ruffle at the neck and, for her it had been the most grown-up item she'd ever owned.

Kyle had obviously thought so too, a frown marring her brow as she noted the way the cheap nylon fabric had clung to her chest. That day, that blouse had been the start of Kyle's obsession with meeting her from school. Her father withdrew into the background, his increasing dependence on the oxygen cylinders littering the house almost going unnoticed as she blossomed from girl to woman.

She sat back, closing her thoughts off to those unsavoury memories, memories that still hurt so much after all this time. It was only then she remembered the letter she still hadn't opened. She'd propped it up on the mantelpiece and forgotten about it. Now it was time to find out why her mother had abandoned her. Oliver had muttered something about last-minute gravy but, whatever the reason for his sudden absence, she appreciated the space he was so obviously giving her.

Two minutes it took; just two minutes to walk across the room, slit the envelope open with shaking fingers and have her whole life come toppling down. Her mother, the one person hard-wired to love her from birth, had loved another more.

She'd only married her father when she'd found out she was pregnant. But not only that, she was pregnant by another man, a man who'd sworn he'd divorce his wife. But the divorce never happened. The same week she discovered she was pregnant, his wife announced her own pending stork visit.

I didn't know what to do. I was loved by both men but was only in love with Arthur, a man who was irretrievably tied to a woman he could never love. After the birth, he came for me and I admit I was weak. He was rich, handsome, and titled – how could I do anything other than follow? He bought me the cottage, and he visited when he could. He would have married me if things had been different. I'm so sorry…

Holly's hands shook as she read the last sentence.

I wanted so much to take you with me but I couldn't do that to your father. I loved him enough to know that it would be the finish of him…

She sighed, folding the letter back inside the envelope before stuffing it into her briefcase along with the plans for Lady Nettlebridge's ballroom. It was all too little, too late. This Arthur person meant nothing to her. He hadn't been a father, a dad. Her true father was the man she still grieved for. The only good thing about all of this was he'd never learnt the truth because her mother was right about that. It would have killed him.

Sitting back down in front of the shoebox she pulled it closer but now instead of searching for photos of her mother, she searched for photos of the man that might be her father. There was nothing of any relevance apart from the letter and that horrid photo still in her hand, a photo she'd like to rip to shreds.

She replaced the lid gently and picked up her glass, aware of a pair of grey eyes staring at her from the other side of the room.

'I'm sorry, I was miles away. The photo, I haven't seen it in years.'

'It doesn't do you justice.'

'I'm sorry?'

'The photo, you're better looking than that.'

'Oh, come on. I'm twenty years older.' B*ut still as young and inexperienced,* a little voice screamed in her head. *Still the naive innocent thing with big eyes and a big chest.*

'True, although my opinion stands, Holly. But then there'd be something seriously wrong if I preferred a young inexperienced girl to a woman, now, wouldn't there?' He stood up and offered his hand. 'Enough of this. I've spent all day slaving over a hot stove and here we are chatting. Come on – it will spoil.'

The chicken was a little dry and the sprouts a little over-cooked not that they noticed. Once that first bite of chilli hit the back of their throat, they hit the carafe of water as if it was rationed. With tears streaming down their cheeks they both agreed on ice cream for afters and left the carefully laid out cheese board for another day.

Making their way across the room they collapsed onto the sofa. There was coffee and port, and the soft lilting melody of something he'd chosen at random from the pile of CD's in the corner.

'Well, that was an alternative Christmas Day and my first without any presents.'

'Ha, unlucky you. I have one, not that I've opened it,' she said, her eyes closed against the dim flickering light.

'You must open it. I insist.'

'Why?' she opened one eye before closing it again. 'Why must I open it? It's something to look forward to.'

'God, stop being so bloody efficient. You have to open it. It's unluck…'

'It's unlucky? To whom is it unlucky? Doctors aren't meant to tell lies you know. You'll be telling me Santa visits next.'

He just stared back in silence before saying, 'I'm not taking no for an answer. Someone's gone to the trouble to think you're worth a present, Holly. Where is it, somewhere in your room?'

She sat up, her eyes wide. 'No, really. I don't want to...' But she was speaking to his retreating back.

It only took him seconds to return with the package, its shiny paper flickering in the reflected firelight. 'Here, catch,' he said, throwing it in her lap before reclaiming his glass and raising it to his lips. 'A toast. To you, Holly, and all your Christmases to come.'

Her eyes dipped towards his before drifting back to the present, her fingers starting to peel back the sticky tape.

Her abhorrence of colour was a joke in the office so she knew that whatever Clare had decided to buy her it wouldn't be black. Never that, as the wrapping fell away and diaphanous pink silk drifted through her hands; a shade reminiscent of the blouse in the photo. Her fingers curled, crushing the fabric between clenched fists, her eyes misting with tears, but not with tears of either sorrow or joy. These were tears of regret at a life lost; her life. If she hadn't met Kyle, if only she hadn't seen that picture and then read those words she'd have loved this piece of flimsy nonsense, but not now...

'It's beautiful, Holly. So beautiful.'

She felt his hands on hers, his fingers unfurling and smoothing before lifting them up to stroke away her tears with the pad of his thumb. 'Don't cry, Holly. There are no tears to be had at such a lovely gift.'

'I don't want it. Throw it in the fire.'

'Really?' His eyebrows arched. 'Now that would be a shame. You really don't want it?'

'No, take it away. I never wear colours and certainly not pink,' her eyes flickering back to the shoebox and the photograph before shifting determinedly towards the flames.

'Well, if you really don't want it. I'll have it. I'm sure I can think of someone deserving who'd love something so beautiful.'

Their eyes clashed. 'Be my guest. I'm sure you have a bevy of beauties just queuing up for your attentions. There are all those nurses pandering to your every desire for a start. *Oh doctor, would you like the forceps or the scalpel?*' she mimicked.

'If I didn't know better, I'd say you were jealous, but then you'd have to have a heart instead of that block of ice in your chest.' He looked at her, his hands gripping onto the nightgown for dear life. 'Who was it that caused the damage? Your father, your husband, or are you just a mean-hearted bitch used to taking while giving nothing in return?'

The face she lifted was stony-white. 'The latter, of course. You'd better go to your room. I'll clear up here.'

She started piling up plates before carrying them into the kitchen, all the time aware of him standing watching before finally turning on his heel. Better he thought her a bitch than know the truth. Her mother had abandoned her at birth and, after Kyle, there'd been no one. She wasn't about to let herself get hurt again.

She heard the door of the shower slam and realised she'd been holding her breath. Letting it out between clenched teeth, she started filling the sink before reaching for the scourer, pleased now that he'd used every dish and pot. It would take her hours, but anything to keep her mind from her thoughts.

He hadn't touched her, apart from with his eyes and then his hands but that was enough as she recalled the frisson of excitement as he'd wiped away her tears. If she didn't know better, she'd have been tricked into believing he cared but that would be impossible. She dropped the scourer back in the sink and, reaching up a soapy hand, smoothed it over her face, tracing the path left by his fingers.

He hadn't grabbed her like those men; those husbands and partners who'd tried it on while their wives and girlfriends were occupied with colour swatches and fabrics. He hadn't tried to fondle, to touch her in any way and now…and now she wished he had because then she could relegate him to that place in her mind where she shoved all the undesirable men she came across. At work it was easy, more than easy. She made them pay through the nose for their behaviour by persuading their partners to choose not just the most expensive designs but the most outlandish. But with him, now, there was nothing she could do except perhaps lock herself in her bedroom until he left.

With the last dish dried and the glassware shining from an enthusiastic polish, she popped on the kettle. She'd spotted a tin of instant chocolate in the cupboard, which might just be the thing she needed to tip her into sleep. Heaping the spoon she realised with a shock she was being watched and, despite her best efforts, ended up spilling most of the powder onto the counter.

She spoke without lifting her head. 'Would you like a hot chocolate, I'm just making one?'

'Is that what it's called?' He laughed, his hand covering hers before removing the spoon. 'I'll make it if you do me a favour?'

'A favour, what sort of fav...?' She looked then and wished she hadn't, her cheeks flaming scarlet. Instead of being dressed in his shirt and trousers all he was wearing was a low-slung towel draped from his hips.

She'd never been this close to a nude man, which was probably why her pulse ratcheted up quite a few notches, even as she caught her lower lip between her teeth and bit down hard. What favour could he want from her except the obvious and, the way she was suddenly feeling, she was pretty sure he could persuade her to change her answer to a yes.

'A favour?' she finally managed.

'Er—yes.'

Was that a blush slashing across his cheeks? Surely not, as she dragged her eyes to his chin. His chin was safe, sort of. Okay, so he had the most amazing jawline and the firmest lips but it was a darn sight safer staring at his chin than almost any other part of his anatomy.

'I'm not sure I can cope with wearing the same clothes again unless they're clean. If you wouldn't mind—?'

Her brain was being particularly slow. Was it her imagination or had he just asked permission to walk around naked? And then she noticed the bundle of clothes he had clutched in his hand and she felt her cheeks flame all over again.

'Oh, of course. Here, let me.'

She took the pile and, stuffing them into the washing machine conveniently situated next to the fridge, spent the next few minutes fiddling around with powder, conditioner and settings until the muffled noises coming from the drum meant she couldn't stay any longer hiding from the weight of his stare.

He was sitting at the kitchen table nursing his mug and she had very little choice other than to join him.

'There's a tumble drier too, so they'll be ready for you in the morning.'

'Thank you,' his hand brushing his still-damp hair off his brow. 'Look, I'd like to apologise about earlier. God, I seem to spend most of my time upsetting you.'

'It's not you, never think that.' She sighed and, for the first time, admitted something she'd never admitted to even herself. 'I know I'm all messed up about how I look; perhaps I'm in need of a good plastic surgeon.'

'You don't need anything I can offer you.'

'What?'

'Holly, I think you're getting me mixed up with a cosmetic surgeon...'

'There's a difference?' her eyes widening.

'There's a difference,' his voice soft. 'I deal with people following catastrophic events like road traffic accidents, or those poor souls with the worst kind of congenital abnormalities. Changing people's looks, just because they think they'd be happier with a different nose or a larger chest...well, whilst admirable, that's not what I do and, if I might be so bold, you don't need the services of either. At worst, you might need a psychiatrist to talk some sense into you, or perhaps a different man to live with. Body confidence is a state of mind in most cases and BDD can be a serious condition if not treated carefully.'

'BDD?'

'Body Dysmorphic disorder, a distorted image of all or part of a person's body - Something I'm beginning to think you may be suffering from. Just look at you? You're in your prime with the most amazing body and yet all you can do is hide away behind a wall of baggy black.'

He stood up, taking his drink with him. 'I've said enough, more than enough. It's not my field of expertise, after all. Good night.'

She heard him go. She heard his footsteps recede down the hall and then the door close gently to his room. But only part of her registered him leaving as she mulled over the conversation.

Is that what he thought of her? After all, despite his words he was an expert on body image, maybe not in the same field but he'd be bound to recognise a related medical condition.

She pushed herself away from the table, her hot chocolate left untouched, and made her way back into the lounge. So, he thought her someone in need of psychiatric help, did he? Great, bloody great. She was beginning to really like him as a person as well as liking him as a man. She closed her mind off to any other words akin to like. Love was a four letter word to someone with her history and one she wouldn't use lightly, if at all. She also closed her mind to her earlier thoughts of having his babies. She liked him. She fancied him. That was all.

She stripped the lid off the shoebox and strew the photos across the table, picking up pictures at random. Those of her as a baby with the cutest kiss curl draped across her forehead and that podgy skin rucked at the wrists and ankles. She'd been a fat baby, a chubby child and then a skinny teen, racehorse lean but still with her signature green eyes twinkling out of the photos. Eyes she must have inherited from her father. And then the photos dwindled as she'd grown. The annual school photos of her muffled up in her navy uniform, hiding her burgeoning figure from the eyes of the camera, were all that was left apart from that final one.

Tracing her finger over her outline she remembered she'd been teased by her friends for being flat-chested, teasing turning to bullying when puberty finally kicked into overdrive. And then there was Kyle, always waiting in the wings. The big brother she'd never had. Shirley and her father had never officially tied the knot, which was probably the only thing she'd been thankful for in the end. After his death and after the annulment, they'd been left with nothing. Would Kyle have married her without his mother pushing him from behind? Of course he wouldn't. He'd have won his bet in a much less honourable fashion than professing his undying love in front of all of his mates.

She gathered together the mass of photos, plonking them back into the box any old how, before walking around the room to check the door was secure and all the lamps were switched off. She lingered then, her eyes drawn to the fire still burning brightly in the stove. The snow had past, hopefully for good just as the wind had dwindled to nothing. By tomorrow the thick rolls of white would start to melt but their memory would live on as a reminder of the day, a day she'd never forget but for all the wrong reasons. Yesterday she'd had a dad and a loving mother taken before her time. Today she'd been left with nothing and, if he was to be believed, she was also in need of psychiatric help.

No, the word whispered from dry lips. She didn't have this distorted view of herself. She wasn't crazy and she didn't have BDD. What she did have was a heightened awareness of what people, men in particular, thought of her. If she could just learn not to mind what other people thought surely this must be the first step in her road to recovery?

Making her way to the stairs, her eyes snagged on something pink and she crossed the room a second time to pick up the night dress. He was right; it was beautiful, so beautiful as she let the fabric pool between her fingers before hugging it to her chest. Her recovery, if that was the word, started now.

Chapter Ten

It was always the same dream and it was starting to bore him. The only problem being it wasn't a dream, it was a nightmare. Three months of reliving that awful day over and over again was starting to take its toll on both his mind and his body.

Doctors weren't perfect. They made mistakes as often as the next person and, these days, they were made to pay the price in the courtroom. But this time the only mistake he'd made was to feel sympathy for the parents of those twins, the conjoined twins he'd so foolishly thought he could save. He'd known more than probably any surgeon living that the chances of any kind of a positive outcome from the surgery were slim at best but he'd been their last hope.

The surgery had gone better than he'd expected under the circumstances. He was applauded by the media as the hero of the hour and hugged by the parents until it had all gone so horribly wrong on that third day. Within twenty-four hours he had not one but two deaths on his hands and he'd been vilified in the media ever since.

He lay there, trapped in his thoughts. He'd lost patients before, what doctor of his age hadn't? But not like this. Not in the glare of the world press, and not just one death but two. How could he continue to operate when, every time he looked down at his hands, all he saw was the image of those babies?

He hadn't been able to face work since so he had nothing to do with his time. Oh, there was a lot to do except that, as a busy in-demand surgeon, he employed an estate manager to oversee Worton and a housekeeper and Chauffeur/handyman to oversee his London apartment. He had nothing to do other than drink and remember, both as destructive to his mental health as they were to his physical.

That's why he'd agreed to drive her, the only reason. It was something to do that was different; something to stretch his mind and his body so that when he fell into bed at night he'd have the blessed relief that sleep provided. He couldn't believe it when it had actually worked. He'd woken up this morning clearer in mind and body than he'd felt in months - and he hadn't dreamt. He'd remained hopeful that his nightmare was over, that he could now start to rebuild instead of self-destruct. He'd remained hopeful until just now, lying there in the semi-darkness with his heart thumping and his head filled with ugly images.

He hadn't slept until last night because, in truth, downing half a bottle of whiskey before collapsing in a drunken stupor each evening wasn't the kind of rest he needed. He didn't know how he even managed to crawl into bed each night with his head on the pillow and the duvet wrapped up to his neck. All he ever remembered of the evenings was the sofa and something inane playing out on the television. He suspected…no, he was 99 percent sure that Parker manhandled him across the apartment. But he could never be sure and his manservant's denial was absolute. However, as he didn't believe in fairies and any and all other conclusions freaked him out, he made sure that this year Parker's Christmas box matched his dedication.

So what had happened to change that? He thought on a grimace as he pushed himself to sitting. He hadn't drunk anything like his recent daily quota and they hadn't fallen back to sleep that second time until the small hours. But, for some reason, the comfort she'd provided couldn't be replicated by inferior imitations as he recalled the bottle of wine they'd had with their meal and the pillow he'd been hugging to his chest.

He'd woken first on Christmas morning, not that he'd ever admit it to her. The sharp sunlight reflecting off the snow had woken him with a start. He was lying on his side, tucked up against her back like a kitten burrowing against its mother for warmth but it was the position of his hand that had given him cause for concern. Somehow during the night it had taken up residence against something tantalisingly round and soft. Whilst part of his brain remained in denial as to the inappropriateness of such behaviour with someone who was

68

still pretty much a stranger, the other part allowed him full reign on his suddenly improper thoughts until common sense kicked in. If she woke up and found him in such a position, delightful as it was, he'd have a great deal of explaining to do and there was no way he was going to be able to produce the right kind of excuse.

He found her attractive, what fully functioning man wouldn't? But it wasn't in his game plan to get involved with anyone when the rest of his life was such a disaster zone.

Standing abruptly, he headed for the door, trying to excuse his thoughts. The bed they'd shared, with the lingering trace of her scent, was just too close for his comfort. He needed sleep, not reminders of a woman with the largest 'Keep Off' sign he'd ever come across. He knew she was married, he'd known from the beginning but now he also knew she was divorced – it didn't help.

He wandered into the kitchen only to find that the sole focus of his thoughts had beaten him to it.

He took one look at her bundled up in her coat and nearly fled for the hills except that the said-same hills were covered in snow and he'd probably freeze to death. He was nearly freezing to death as it was, standing there in his towel, a towel he'd only wrapped around his waist, at the very last minute, not for a moment thinking she'd be anywhere other than tucked upstairs in the land of nod.

'What's this, the Polruan insomniac's society?' he quipped, pulling a mug from the shelf and pouring a cupful from the pot in the centre.

'Yep, it's a very exclusive club, mind,' she quipped back, throwing him a small smile. 'Your clothes are dry by the way,' as she tilted her head to the hook on the back of the door.

'You didn't need to iron them.' He slipped his arms into the sleeves, casually fastening a couple of buttons before sitting down and picking up his mug.

'I enjoy ironing.'

'Really?' His look astonished, as he focused on the sharp creases running from shoulder to cuff just the way he liked them. 'I didn't think anyone enjoyed ironing. Even Mrs Grant sends out my shirts because she says I'm far too fussy.'

'Oh, that's great. Now he tells me. First I find I'm holed up with a plastic surgeon and then I find he's fussy.'

'We prefer the term reconstructive surgeon,' he interrupted with a frown.

'Whatever.' It was her turn to furrow her brow. 'When do you need to get back, you must have patients… it's not as if it's nine to five or anything?'

'I've been…off sick.'

'But you're well now, aren't you?' her eyes wide. 'Nothing serious I hope, or catching for that matter?'

'No, nothing like that.' He raked his hand through his hair, suddenly reluctant to meet her gaze, or was it just he was reluctant to share with her what a mess he'd made of his life? Probably a little of both.

'I was off with stress, if you must know. I lost a couple of patients and…I found it difficult to…' the words out before he'd even planned to say them. Words he had no idea how to finish. He looked down to where she had reached across and taken his hand between hers, her skin just as silky soft as he remembered.

'You don't have to say anymore, you know. I can't begin to understand what that must be like. I've lost my dad and now my mother…'

'You don't understand,' his fingers curling around hers. 'I made a mistake in operating, a mistake I'll have to live with. I knew it was pointless but their parents were desperate. They blamed me in the end and they were probably right because I gave them hope, you see? I gave them hope and then I took it away.'

He felt her hand stiffen under his. 'I don't understand, I thought you said you lost two patients—?'

'I did. Conjoined twins.'

'Oh, God.' She pulled her hand free only to move it to her mouth, her expression saying it all.

She was horrified, more than horrified and now he wished more than anything that he'd lied. He could have lied. He could have said he'd broken a limb or something. He could have told her virtually anything other than the truth but it was too late for that now. He'd failed that family, he'd failed himself and now he'd hurt her, too. He should have remembered she was a lay-person and that she'd view things through rose-coloured glasses instead of the harsh frames of reality.

'I remember. It was in all the papers. Oh God,' she repeated. You're that Lord Ivy person…Here I am calling you Oliver when I should be calling you sir…' her voice trailing off. 'You should have said, and those poor babies and their distraught parents; the surgery that no one else was prepared to undertake because of—?'

'Yes, well.' He stood up, pushing away from the table before heading to the sink and rinsing his cup, his mind in free-fall as memory overlaid memory and then emotion took over.

Her reaction was the last straw in a field full of hay bales. It was the straw that broke the camel's back, although what a camel was doing in an English hayfield was one of life's unanswerable mysteries. He'd certainly be clutching at straws if he thought for one moment there'd be a happy ending to this interlude, as hay bale idioms swirled around his head like tumbleweed in a bad Western.

His hands gripped the edge of the sink, his knuckles bone-white as a pile-driving migraine decided to slam his brain against his skull and nausea built. He was about to embarrass himself big time in front of this woman and there was absolutely nothing he could do about it as the first in a torrent of tears plopped onto the back of his hand before slithering to the floor in a silent plop. It wasn't his hands shaking now, it was his whole body. He needed to get out of there, out of her presence but he suddenly couldn't move. If he let go of the sink, his legs would finally lose the running battle they had with his muscles. He needed…He didn't know what he needed except perhaps for her to realise that he couldn't cope with her seeing him like this. Men were meant to be the stronger of the species. They weren't meant to turn into shivering pain-wracked wrecks at the first hurdle.

'Go, just go,' he finally managed, his eyes scrunched closed in a half-hearted attempt at pushing back the tears.

He felt her hand on his back and then she was prising his fingers free before pulling him into her arms, her hands rhythmically stroking his back.

'I'm not going anywhere and you'd better get used to it,' she whispered, rising up on tippy-toes to press a kiss against his damp cheek. 'I don't know anything about anything but I do know it couldn't have been your fault,' she added, leaning back and brushing away his tears. 'Just look at the way you insist on your shirts being so perfect? You're a lord from the top of your head to the tip of your shoes. Just look at how you managed to get us to Polruan, and in the middle of a snow storm, when driving isn't your thing? There's no way you'd drop the ball in the operating theatre. There's no way you'd drop any ball unless you had no choice. If you couldn't save them, then no one could but at least you had the guts to try.' She drew him closer, her head resting on his chest as her hands continued soothing across his back in the lightest of touches. 'Being emotional is nothing to be ashamed of. In fact, I'd think less of you if you were one of those domineering alpha males who never let a tear escape or a soppy word pass their lips. Men cry silent tears…there's no shame in sharing them.'

He found her pulling on his hand and leading him upstairs in a dull parody of what it could have been like with her in another life, another time; if he'd been another man. But now wasn't the time for such thoughts. Now was the time to curl up into as tiny a ball as his six-foot-three frame would allow and try to sleep.

She helped him off with his shirt as if he was a toddler and not a grown man before tucking the duvet up around his neck. Did he imagine the brief, cool kiss pressed against his forehead before she turned the lights out and climbed in beside him? Did he imagine hearing her coat whisper to the floor before she hugged him to her breast? He imagined nothing as dreams tangled with reality and sleep drew him under the cover of sweet darkness.

He awoke to a re-enactment of yesterday. Just like yesterday the space beside him was empty, apart from a hint of pink peeking out from under the pillow. He let out a groan then as his memory banks scrolled back and he remembered the feel of soft silk against his skin. She'd worn it and he'd missed it – just great, bloody great.

'Are you going to stay up there forever?' the sound of her voice trailing up the stairs.

'Just coming,' he replied, pulling on the clothes she'd left on the end of the bed. She'd even washed his socks and his boxers, but he didn't allow himself to dwell on the issue as the smell of toast sent his stomach rumbling.

She was wearing black again was his first thought, a different black, it was true but black all the same. This time she'd chosen a long, black skirt, teaming it with a black shirt and thick, mohair cardigan buttoned up to the neck. She looked like someone on her way to a funeral; apart from the fact she'd left her hair to fall loose over her shoulders. She had pretty hair. *She had pretty everything* was his second thought, a thought mingled with the regret of not having stayed awake long enough to sneak a peek at how good she must have looked in that pink.

'The snow's melting,' the sound of her voice interrupting his musings and making him look out of the window at the vastly changing scene outside. Yes, there was still snow; bucketful's of snow but also the sight of green on the treetops and a glimmer of grey where path met flower borders.

'It is, isn't it? I should be able to leave later.'

'Do you think? Tomorrow might be better, the roads, you know,' as she turned back to the worktop. 'You wouldn't want to risk another journey like Christmas Eve. I don't mind putting you up for another night, and anyway, you make a passable hot-water-bottle. A little noisy it's true but…'

'What, are you saying I snore?'

'Only a little, it was quite cute actually; like being tucked up next to a little piglet with a sore throat.'

'I'll give you piglet.' With one step he was standing in front of her, his hands gently encircling her shoulders as he stared down into those mesmerising eyes. He could drown in those pools of green even as he worked on words instead of kisses. He still wasn't sure what their relationship footing was but she had asked him to stay the night so it could all change. For now he'd make do with being her friend; a friend with sleeping privileges.

'I want to say thank you for yesterday. I don't normally fall apart, especially in front of someone like you.'

73

'Someone like me?'

'Yes, someone warm, soft and very female,' his lips grazing across her forehead, her eyelids, her cheeks before finally hovering over her lips, his hands shifting from her shoulders to cradle her face as his fingers stroked the smooth skin on her cheeks.

'I'm not even sure how you kept it together for so long.'

'I wasn't keeping anything together, Holly. Everything was falling apart,' he whispered, his fingers shifting from her cheeks to her hair. 'It's only since meeting you I've been able to reach any kind of perspective. You're my lucky mascot.'

'I'm a very hungry, lucky mascot.'

He stepped back, taking the hint offered, his gaze lingering. 'Well—em—I think I'll see if I can get the car started now that I can actually see it again.'

'Have your breakfast first and...' she touched his arm briefly. 'What about a walk down to the sea? There may be a pub open for lunch.'

Chapter Eleven

Polruan
Boxing Day

It was a day without equal, a day to be remembered; a day that went straight into the memory banks to be filed under *the best day ever.*

After breakfast and after Oliver had managed to clear his car and start the engine, they wrapped up in a hotchpotch of clothing before tramping down the hill, the pristine white snow of yesterday now not quite so pristine. The air was crisp and cold but the temperature above freezing. There were signs all around that, by tomorrow, Christmas and its winter wonderland would slide into that grey-black dirty slush stage. But for now there was still enough snow for the inevitable snowball fight along the way and, with laughter chiming out across the valley, they slipped back into easy companionship, or should that be truce? The memory of that kiss was there peering in at the edges; a look, a touch, a blush, a lingering awkwardness...

Polruan was small, quaint and rustic; a place out of this world where time stood suspended across the centuries. Unlike other more touristy parts of Cornwall, for some reason the tourist industry seemed to have forgotten all about this little slice of paradise. The post office had more in common with a thick-walled cottage than a sub-branch whilst the narrow, cobbled streets preserved a quintessential rusticity of a bygone era.

By mutual consent, they pushed open the door of one of the pubs and, over a glass of wine, decided on thick bowls of vegetable soup served with freshly-baked warm rolls before popping into the general store and stocking up on fresh bread and milk.

They knew they had this evening. They knew, with each successive look and with each touch, there was something pending, something unfinished in their relationship. They were two strangers thrown together and yet not strangers. Tomorrow would come soon enough. Tomorrow he'd leave, but he wouldn't leave her, he couldn't. She'd entwined herself around his heart very much like his namesake even as he wondered what her reaction would be if he was to propose. He could do very little about his name, but to go from Holly Branch to Holly Ivy surely wasn't that much of a leap? He could always change his name, of course, although Oliver Branch was probably as bad, if not worse…He'd think about it later, first there was this evening followed by tonight.

Dusk was starting to fall by the time they pushed open the door to the cottage, thankful they'd decided to bank up the wood burner. Following the usual pattern of male/female domesticity, Holly headed for the kitchen and the kettle while Oliver hunched down on the hearth to add more logs from the dwindling pile.

'We should have enough for tonight but I'll chop some before I go.' He looked up and caught her watching him from the doorway, a strange expression on her face even as he glanced down at the phone in her hand. His phone, the one he'd decided to charge before they went on their walk.

Chapter Twelve

'**T**here's a call for you, Lord Ivy.'

'What? Why are you being so formal?' his eyes now on her face and her sudden pallor.

'Well, that's your name isn't it? Lord Ivy, the Earl of Worton, unless I've got it wrong. Your father's name was Arthur?' She spoke the name as if it was an illness, a disease even. A deadly epidemic she was scared to catch let alone be in the same room as.

'Yes, but I don't understand. Where does my father fit into all of this?' He spread his hands. 'Look, I'm not sure what's going on but…you say there's a call?' his gaze now on the phone still in her hand. He couldn't begin to guess what had gotten into her so he decided not to try. There was a call. It must be urgent. That was all he could process at the moment.

As he reached to take it, their fingers touched and she drew back as if he'd hit her. He wanted to question her then but he didn't. He'd attend to the call and then he'd tackle the situation, even as he wondered what the situation was. What could have happened in the last couple of minutes to change everything? He'd been in paradise; now he'd descended straight to hell.

'Ivy here.'

'Ah, sir, at last. I've been trying to contact you since yesterday.'

'Sorry, Parker. The lines have been down with the snow.'

'You didn't say you'd be away, sir?' the sound of displeasure clear to hear from his tone.

'It was a last minute thing. Is everything alright? You and Mrs Parker had a nice Christmas?'

'Yes, sir. That's not the reason I'm phoning.' There was a long pause. 'There's another one. You're needed.'

He leant forward, gripping the edge of the windowsill. 'Another one?' his voice now whisper soft. 'Another what?' he continued even though he knew.

'Another set of them twins. They were born on Christmas Eve. You're needed urgently, sir.'

He found her sitting on the side of the bed, staring into space, and sat down beside her, careful to leave a little gap between them.

'You should have told me?'

'Look, Holly. I can't begin to know what's going on here but I have to leave. They're sending a helicopter.'

She turned then and he noted the depth of despair lurking in the back of her eyes. 'What is it, dearest? What's happened?' as he went to draw her to him.

'Don't touch me,' she folded her arms across her chest as if to ward off any contact, her face paler, if that was possible, than the snow lingering outside the windows.

'I thought you could come with me—? But I was obviously wrong.'

He stood up and walked to the window before walking back and kneeling by her feet, his hands by his side as he studied her face as if memorising it.

'There's another set of twins; in America. They've chartered a flight from Gatwick. Won't you come and we can talk?' He paused, his hands now on her knees and he felt her trembling, just as he too was starting to shiver. He was scared. No, he was terrified.

'Holly, sweetheart, I don't think I can do this without you by me. You make me... I'm only at peace when you're with me. I want you. No, that's not true,' as he dragged his hand through his hair. 'I think I'm falling in love with you and I had hoped you felt the same way.' His voice trailed off and, into the silence, the sound of a helicopter in the distance filtered through as if heralding the death-knell of their relationship.

'I have to go even though I don't want to, I don't want to leave you like this,' his eyes on her face. 'There'll be someone to pick up the car at some point. I'm sorry for any inconvenience I've caused,' he ended, in an attempt to rebuild the defences she'd smashed through with her lips and her kindness.

She started. Whether it was his words or the sound of someone banging on the door but suddenly she was jumping to her feet and scrabbling around for her shoes and coat before turning to him, her expression blank.

'You know as well as I do that you're in no fit state to operate. How could they do this to you?'

'There's no one else.'

'There's no one else in the whole wide world able to—?' she watched as he shook his head. 'So I'll come with you but only for the twins. Nothing more. Promise me you won't try to...?' He watched her swallow what looked like a sudden boulder in her throat, her eyes careful to avoid his. 'Promise me, God damn it?'

He'd been offered a reprieve, a reprieve with so many strings he'd never be able to untangle the knots. But he wasn't complaining as he followed her down the stairs and watched as she checked her bag for her passport. He'd find out what the problem was on the flight and then...and then he'd take her to bed.

He didn't remember the flight. All he remembered was her grim determination as she reclined her seat beside his and closed her eyes, but he wasn't fooled. She wasn't asleep if the uneven pattern of her breathing was anything to go by. She was faking it and if she was able to fake sleep for hours on end what else had she been able to fake as he remembered her passion during that kiss? He was mad to have brought her but he couldn't contemplate leaving her behind. He'd teased by calling her his lucky mascot but that's what he truly believed of her. She made him whole again after all those months of isolation and despair. She was the other half of him and...He finally closed his eyes on the truth, the truth that had snuck up from nowhere and attacked his heart like a sledgehammer. He'd fallen in love with her and it looked very much as if she suddenly couldn't stand the sight of him. Something had happened in the time she'd gone to boil the kettle and the phone call but he couldn't for the life of him work it out. He was pretty sure it had something to do with his name, although how could his name change anything…?

He pulled out his notebook and pen from his inside breast pocket and started scribbling notes of all the things that didn't make any sense. It wasn't a long list but there was that name of her mother's, and then his father's as his mind went into overdrive. He'd always suspected something like this but he'd never bothered to look into it and now he wished he had…He glanced at his watch. It was still only the small hours in the UK but, as soon as he could, he had some phone calls to make.

Instead of breakfast when they eventually landed at JFK airport he dropped her off at The Hilton with a pile of dollars he'd just withdrawn from the cashpoint inside the airport terminal.

'I don't need your money, Oliver.'

'I don't care, Holly. You're here because of me with no clothes except what you're standing up in…'

'What about you, huh?' she interrupted, grabbing her bag from his hands. 'You're in the same boat, without as much as a toothbrush or…'

'I'll be wearing scrubs, but if you could grab me a couple of things, I'd be grateful.' He bent towards her mouth only to change direction and press a kiss on her cheek. 'Humour me, sweetheart, just this once. I should be back at the hotel sometime around lunch.'

Chapter Thirteen

New York
December 27th

She'd never been to New York before.

She'd never been anywhere really apart from Berkshire, London and, now, Polruan because she couldn't count the two weeks she'd spent in Italy holed up in her hotel bedroom as any sort of holiday. After that disaster, she hadn't bothered. If holidays could be that bad, she certainly wasn't in a rush to repeat the experience.

She worked, she went home and she went on the very occasional date, but only the ones she really couldn't avoid. There was never a third date and rarely a second.

She was self-sufficient, or at least she had been until she'd tapped on his car window. Now her perfectly tailored life was a disaster zone. She was on the other side of the world acting paid companion and potential special friend to Lord Ivy, who, if her mother's letter was to be believed, also happened to be her brother. Her half-brother it was true but still, in the eyes of the church and the world at large, wrong on all levels.

She loved him. There, she'd finally admitted it. She loved him, but not as a brother; as a lover, as a best friend. As someone she wanted to spend the rest of her life with and now…She loved him too much to desert him now but later, when the operation was over she'd…

She clambered aboard the subway, collapsing onto one of the seats, welcoming the sudden interruption to her thoughts as her eyes snagged on the newspaper being rustled by the man opposite.

'World renowned British surgeon called in to save twins - last ditch attempt'

Her eyes filled with sudden tears. She couldn't even escape her thoughts here; she'd never escape them, and what about him? He couldn't operate; he just couldn't if there was no hope. Who the hell did he think he was anyway, playing God like this?

The doors opened at the next stop and she jumped off, uncaring now as to where she was. She'd meant to go shopping and she would for toothpaste and the like but any ideas of strolling along Fifth Avenue and searching for a new shirt and tie for him deserted her. She'd grab a coffee and head back to the hotel and try and talk some sense into him.

Wandering onto 59th Street, she found herself outside Bloomingdales, a shop she'd actually heard of and, walking through the doors, headed straight for the café; coffee first as she hadn't had either supper or breakfast and then she'd buy toiletries.

She meandered around the store in a daze. She'd bought toiletries for both of them including shaving foam and a razor, having no idea if he dry or wet shaved. There was underwear too as she tried not to blush at the thought of buying her first pair of boxers at the age of thirty-six. But at least she knew he liked red as she remembered back to that morning in the kitchen. She even threw in a shirt, similar to the one she'd washed, and a pair of jeans, which would probably be the wrong size but it was meant to be the thought that counted.

Glancing down at her uniform of black she had a sudden desire for something more colourful, something purple or perhaps green?

She went mad then. She still had a handful of his money but that remained untouched in the bottom of her bag as she took her credit card for a walk. After all, she could afford to buy exactly what she wanted and, for the first time since her aborted wedding, she wanted to wear something other than black.

'Madam has such wonderful colouring and the perfect shape.'

She arched an eyebrow at the enthusiasm of the sales assistant as she followed her into the changing room, both arms full of clothes.

Reaching out for the first dress, she dragged it over her head with little enthusiasm but it took just one look in the mirror to fall in love with the green, beaded sleeveless Adrianna Papell, not least because the deep v shaped neckline was offset by a sheer gauze insert, which only hinted at the delights underneath. Of course, she had nowhere to wear it but it was just one of those dresses she had to have. She'd soon added matching shoes to the pile; long, slim-heeled delights that she'd need to pass her test to wear. Jeans came next but not the baggy black pair she'd rescued from the bottom of her wardrobe. These weren't really jeans at all. These were sculptured denims which made her legs go on for ever and did the most amazing thing to her bottom. She teamed them with tight V-necked t-shirts in an assortment of rainbow colours and, her fingers heading for an all-encompassing black cardigan, paused before opting for the same design but this time in baby blue. Underwear came next but instead of the industrial cotton she normally opted for, the sales assistant encouraged her to be bold, not that she needed much encouragement at the delightful array of silks and satins on display.

She came away with a much lighter pocket but also a much lighter heart. She'd get there. She wasn't there yet, but she was on the road to recovery. He'd helped her more that he could ever know and now it was her turn to help him. She'd help him and then she'd walk away because that was the only option open to her as she thought about the thick serviceable pair of pyjamas she'd finally added at the last minute.

Arriving back at the hotel she was surprised to find him pacing the floor of reception.

'Do you know the time?' he demanded, grabbing her shoulders. 'I've been worried out of my mind. I thought something had happened to you…' his voice ringing sharply in her ears even though he kept his tone low.

'Shopping is what's happened to me,' her look wary as she pointed to the pile of bags by her feet. 'Toothpaste and the like.'

She hadn't been aware that time had trickled through her fingers or that the clock was ticking towards three. All she was interested in was the sudden pallor of his face and the way his lips were pulled back in a grim line. There were new lines etched around his eyes that she didn't remember and a restless energy that took her breath. He was obviously under an enormous strain. Her troubles could wait.

'How did it go?' her eyes now tender.

'Not here,' he held her elbow and marched her to the elevator, the other hand making short work of the parcels and bags. 'I've ordered sandwiches in the room.'

Once the doors slid closed she moved away, breaking contact but it was as if she was still held, captivated by the way his gaze framed her face like an artist staring at a masterpiece. The day before yesterday she'd have been amused. Yesterday she'd have been delighted. Today all she felt was a deep sadness scarring her soul for the hurt heading his way.

She hadn't bothered to enquire about the room or rooms, there was little point. She knew whatever he'd booked that they'd end up sharing simply because it seemed to be the only way he could sleep. But, when he opened the door, her eyes widened in surprise because he hadn't just booked a room. He'd booked a suite of rooms. The lounge was probably larger than her whole apartment, but it wasn't the size that took her attention it was the panoramic ceiling-to-floor windows overlooking the New York skyline and the baby grand piano tucked away in the corner.

Who the hell lived like this? She thought, throwing him a worried glance. She was used to luxury but nothing on this grand scale.

There were two doors leading off the lounge, presumably to the bedrooms and *en-suite* bathrooms. But, instead of investigating, she sat down on one of the cream sofas and picked up the teapot with a slightly unsteady hand. The sandwiches were presented threefold on a tiered cake-stand, although she wasn't even sure if they could be called sandwiches. There was certainly no resemblance between these and the ones he'd bought on the motorway service station as she picked up a brie and bacon baby-sized roll. She watched as he loaded his plate like a starving man just back from the desert only to sit beside her and leave his food untouched.

'I want to thank you for coming; I know it's not what you wanted.' He shook his head slightly and looked more like a little boy than anything; a little boy who suddenly didn't understand what was going on, and she couldn't really blame him. Up until yesterday they'd been moving free-fall into some kind of a relationship.

She fought back the feeling of sudden nausea. Their parents had made a mess of things and it looked like they were going to have to pay the price for both her mother and his father's infidelities. But at least she'd found out before anything had happened. She closed her mind to the memory of that kiss; a memory she'd take to her grave.

Looking at his stern face, she realised she needed to offer some kind of an excuse for her behaviour. Not the truth, or at least not yet. She'd write to him when, after…the coward's way out but it was the only way she knew how to end things. She couldn't lie to him, even now, so she'd just go with the truth; a different truth, the truth about what had happened before they'd even met.

'You were going to tell me about the twins? I don't know how the parents must be coping. There was something on the front of the paper when I was on the subway.'

His eyes clashed with hers and she was shocked at the sight of his expressionless face.

'Parents, that's a laugh. One parent, a sixteen-year-old girl. The father dumped her as soon as he found out. There aren't even any grandparents,' his face rigidly fixed to the floor. 'I'm just waiting on a colleague flying in from Dublin, a fellow surgeon. He was with me the last time and he's agreed to come on board, even though his wife is nearly due.' He raised his head and stared at her. 'The operation has to happen now. One of them isn't doing too good so it's now, or it will be too late. I don't like to ask but if you wouldn't mind staying just for a couple of days? Just to get me over the...' His eyes closed and, looking down at his arms, she noticed a slight tremor even though he tried to disguise it by clenching his fists.

Placing her cup and saucer back down on the table she reached out a hand and gently closed her fingers around his.

'Come on, we're both suffering from exhaustion, let's have a lie down.'

He pulled out of her grasp, his eyes roaming over her face. 'I didn't think you'd want to…? Just having you here is all I ask, that's why I booked a suite.'

'Oliver, there is something I need to tell you,' she sighed in resignation at the difficult conversation ahead but she had to tell him something, and part of the truth would do because she certainly wasn't prepared to tell him the whole truth. 'You know when I said I was divorced, well I lied.'

He pulled away like a scalded cat, his gaze boring down on her.

'What, you're still married? But where is he? Are you a widow? Are there kids?'

'No, I'm not a widow and I'm not married. I've never viewed myself as married, despite the ring,' her eyes now on her hand. 'In fact, I don't know why I wear this thing.' She gripped her fingers around the band of gold before pulling it off and aiming it across the room at the waste paper bin. 'I started annulment proceedings the morning after the wedding.' She swallowed hard. 'I found that the man I married wasn't the man I thought he was, so I left. And I've been scared to…to…' She felt her cheeks burn as her speech dried up.

'You mean you've never? You're still a—?' his eyes wide.

'Well, you're the doctor,' she managed on a sort of laugh. 'I'm not sure whether a thirty-six-year-old could still be termed a virgin but I suppose if the label fits…'

'Oh, honey, why didn't you tell me? It's no big deal to me but to you, for you to have…' he said, trying to pull her into his arms but she took a step back just in time.

'Oliver, I'm embarrassed enough as it is. So let's not talk about it anymore. Let's just say that if you sleep better with me beside you then I'm happy to share your bed but that's all it will be.'

Chapter Fourteen

'Holly, I'd like you to meet Mitch Merrien, We go way back.'

'It's a pleasure to meet you, Holly, although I don't know what you're doing with this old reprobate.'

'I know.' She shook her head in mock annoyance. 'I was all set for a quiet Christmas and then your friend here decided to trap me in deepest, darkest Cornwall for the duration.'

'Wow, that must've been amazing? My wife, Liddy, is always banging on about renting a cottage in Cornwall. It's something we might look into after the baby is born.'

'Well, it's only sitting there empty until I decide what to do with it,' she said with a smile, liking the quietly spoken Irishman on sight. 'Why don't you make use of it? And you can tell me what you think so I can decide whether to sell or rent.'

'Really, that would be amazing, absolutely amazing. Liddy doesn't get out and about much at the moment but it would be something to look forward to, and the baby will be a few months old by the summer.'

'Why don't you let me have her number or email or something and I'll get in touch?'

She watched in amusement as he took out his notebook and pen and started scribbling, although she wasn't quite sure she'd be able to interpret the handwriting any time soon as she glanced down at the paper he'd pushed towards her.

'Do all doctors have bad handwriting then?' she teased.

'Actually, no,' he grinned. 'Your boyfriend here has the most amazingly neat handwriting. He obviously didn't work hard enough at Med School and that's why he's ended up in plastics instead of brain surgery like me,' his hand reaching over and thumping Oliver on the shoulder.

'Ha, bloody ha,' Oliver snapped, rubbing his hand over his arm even as she tried to think up a reply. But he was a lot quicker.

'Actually, Holly is not my girlfriend, Mitch, she's just a friend.'

'Good to know in case I put my size thirteens in it. Talking about friends, Gerry has been asking for you,' Mitch replied, throwing her a quick glance across the table. 'Gerry is our esteemed theatre sister and a valued member of the team but, for some reason, she does seem to think that Oliver is her personal property, and I'm not sure he's man enough to say no. She can be quite forceful.'

'Forceful isn't the word for what Gerry is,' he mumbled under his breath.

Mitch laughed, his eyes again on Holly and her pretty blonde hair, which she'd pulled back into a diamanté hairclip. 'As much as she's good at her job, she scares us blokes and that's a fact. It's a little disconcerting to find the woman you're talking to is actually taller and fitter than you are. She must be six-two and a hundred-and fifty pounds, but a hundred-and-fifty pounds of pure, solid muscle.'

'Surely she can't help her size or her build?' Holly questioned.

'No, of course she can't and we don't really mean to tease. But she can help her attitude, and her attitude stinks. But she is a good nurse; organised, efficient and...'

'In the theatre environment that's all you should be interested in,' she replied softly.

'If only it was as simple as that, dear Holly,' he said, turning back to Oliver and continuing to speak as if she wasn't there. 'She's nice this friend of yours. In fact, she is probably too nice for you. If it wasn't for Liddy and the kids you'd be in for some strong competition.'

'I am still here, you know,' she said, her face struggling not to break into a smile.

She couldn't actually believe she was sitting at the same table with two of the best looking men she'd probably ever seen, both on and off screen. She thought Oliver stunning in a dark, haunted kind of way. He was all sharp angles and shadows, and those silver-grey eyes of his mesmerised her each time she stared into his face. But Mitch was something else altogether; equally tall, equally broad-shouldered. And, if she was honest, he had the edge on handsome. This Liddy was a very lucky woman as she struggled to find something less embarrassing to discuss.

'So how many children have you got?'

'This will be number four, which I think is enough for any man,' he said on a wink. 'We've only been married three years but the first was twins.' He took a quick glance across the table at Oliver. 'When Oliver asked me to get involved with his twin project, I jumped at it.'

'Well, I couldn't think of anybody else foolhardy enough to team up with.'

'Would you look at that? He's gone all modest,' Mitch said in a loud whisper. 'There is no one, and I mean no one else on the planet that can do what Oliver can do with a skull. I'm only the brain surgeon, just there to diathermy off any loose ends and in case any problems crop up but the real skill lies with this man.'

'Okay, okay,' she raised both hands as if trying to ward off any further comments. 'So I know where to go if I'm in need of a good plastic surgeon,' her eyes twinkling. 'But for now all I need is a good night's sleep,' she added, standing up and gathering her bag. 'I'm sure you probably have some gory details to go over and those kinds of nightmares I can do without.'

...

'God, she's some looker that Holly of yours.'

'As I said last night she's not mine. We're just friends.'

'Friends with benefits, or was it my imagination that the receptionist only handed you one key card?'

'You're too clever for your own good, you know that, don't you?' he said, scrubbing between his fingernails with a relentless determination.

'Yep,' a large smirk on his face. 'You just go on believing it.'

They were standing side-by-side in front of the large sinks; dressed in similar, faded green scrubs as they nail brushed their hands and arms until their skin gleamed red. The Fritton twins, as they were called, were even now in the anaesthetic area waiting quietly while the team finished off preparing.

Theatres were busy places, full of the clinking and clattering of trolleys and the sound of hurried footsteps. But today, silence reigned as an unnatural, almost eerie, hush descended. It was always like this on the big day as nerves stretched wire-tight and fear mingled with hope. But today there was more fear and very little hope…

Twin one was a fighter. Only three days old, he'd taken great delight in shaking his fists and giving full-rein to his cries almost as soon as he'd caught sight of the big-wide-world just within his grasp. But twin two was different. Small, quiet and still, his deep blue eyes nevertheless watchful and staring as if he too could sense the fear. The whole team was pulling for both babies but secretly they knew twin one had the better chance.

Mitch and Oliver, the leaders of the thirty-strong team, strolled into the theatre and took up their places at the head of the table, their eyes now on the sleeping faces just visible under all the wires and tubing. Oliver took a moment, just one, to stare down at the twins. Was twin two slightly paler? He'd try to be quick but, by necessity it would be a long job as he flexed his shoulders.

'Are they ready?' Oliver tilted his head to the two anaesthetists.

'Not really, but as ready as they'll ever be.'

'Scalpel, please.'

He glanced down at the blue-handled blade resting on his gloved palm for a second, the steel glinting under the theatre lamps. All was silent apart from the slow whoosh from the machines, the only thing keeping the babies alive. His eyes flickered upwards briefly to the row upon row of fellow doctors imprisoned behind a wall of glass as they watched his every move. His hand was steady. His thoughts blank except for the job in hand as he pressed the tip of the blade into skin. He didn't have time to watch the blood flow red as he reached for the first of the swabs handed to him. He didn't have time to spare a thought for anything as skill, practice and that little bit of instinct that seemed to know just what he should do seconds before it was needed, kicked in.

The operation was over. Sixteen hours later and he was again standing in front of the sinks beside Mitch, flinging away his blood-soaked gloves and gown before pulling down his mask with a long sigh.

'Well done, old man. That went better than we could have hoped under the circumstances.'

All I want is a beer and bed, but I won't,' Oliver replied, the lines around his eyes etched with tiredness.

'They'll want some kind of press release.'

'Well, they can whistle as far as I'm concerned. I'll go and see the mother and then, if they pass the three day mark, I'll think again.' He slapped him on the back before pressing his shoulder briefly. 'Thank you, it was a bit hairy at one point...'

'At one point! There was no point I wasn't scared witless. It was only the unflappable presence of Lord Oliver Ivy that kept me from screaming out the room like a banshee. Remind me, if I'm ever in a crisis to give you a call. Now, go and put Holly out of her misery while I phone Liddy. They won't rest until they know we're at least still standing and that those two mites have made it past stage one.'

Chapter Fifteen

December 30th

The one place she shouldn't be was here. She had no right. He had no right to expect her. She'd have to be both deaf and blind not to hear the talk amongst the team about Lord Ivy's new girlfriend. But it wasn't nasty or malicious. They were a well-meaning bunch. Even Gerry had proven to be a pussycat. It was her that was the sticking point, or at least the lie that she was living and it couldn't go on for much longer.

She couldn't go on for much longer.

She stepped out of the shower before reaching for her brush. She was here because of the twins, only that but reminding herself of that fact was becoming an increasing necessity. She wasn't eating. She wasn't sleeping. She was existing by his side like the dutiful wife she wasn't, ensuring he had everything he needed in order to keep his hands from shaking and his indomitable will from collapsing like that night at the cottage. And she was managing, just about. He was eating everything that she put in front of him and, after the inevitable cuddle, which she couldn't have avoided even if she'd wanted to, he'd slept the sleep of the dead, only to wake refreshed and wonder at her heavy eyes and increasing pallor.

She'd never been in such a position in her life. In truth, she was stuck in her ways and, living alone with only herself to think about, she'd be the first to call herself selfish. She ate what she wanted when she wanted and never had to think about anyone else outside of the work environment. She had enough money to afford the best and, whilst far from a spendthrift, she bought what she wanted when she wanted, within reason. But now she didn't matter. Nothing mattered except helping this tall, quiet almost-stranger function at doing what he was best at. The fact that she'd fallen in love with him was immaterial to almost anything. He didn't know and he'd never know from her lips. She wasn't prepared to tell him about their relationship. She didn't want his money or his title. She didn't want anything from him except the one thing she couldn't have so she'd walk away and make sure she avoided attending any of the same parties. Their paths hadn't crossed before and, now she knew who her nemesis was, she'd make sure they never crossed again.

Chapter Sixteen

How could three days go so fast?

He stood in front of the mirror and tried to flatten his hair, which for some reason wouldn't do what he wanted it to. He wasn't normally interested in how he looked but he thought he'd better make some kind of an effort with the eyes of the world's media again hovering in his direction.

He had a press conference to give, a press conference he hadn't even thought about until this morning when the three day target he's given himself was up.

Twin one, or Mitch as he was now going to be christened, was thriving. He was still being nursed in the special-care-baby-unit and would remain there for many months to come but, all in all, the little bruiser seemed to have taken the operation in his stride. Give him a few months and he'd be meeting and overtaking his milestones, or his brother wasn't called Oliver. He smiled, as he finally gave up on the hair and glanced from the bathroom door to his watch with a frown. Just how long did it take for a woman to stuff her head into a frock anyway even as his thoughts went back to where they'd lingered for the last 72 hours.

Twin two being named after him had come out of the blue and was such an honour. He'd always had a thing for the underdog and little Ollie was certainly that. But he was a plucky little fellow. He'd take a while to catch up to his big brother but, with a bit of luck and perhaps a few more operations, he'd be pretty much like any other boy and, of course, he'd always have his brother to look out for him. His work here was done or it would be after the press conference.

They were booked home on New Year's Day, which only gave him two days to pluck up his courage as his thoughts swung back to the woman who'd stuck by his side for the last four days. Without her, he wouldn't have slept even a wink and as for eating…there were only so many sandwiches he could stomach. She accompanied him to the hospital each morning only to pop back at lunch to drag him away to one of the famed street corner delis. Each evening, instead of nagging to be taken out, she ordered room service knowing, without being told, that he couldn't face being on display in some fancy restaurant. Mitch was made of sterner stuff and he relished in putting on a show with the rest of the team but then he hadn't grown up as an only child. Oliver had always felt awkward around people and, apart from his staff and perhaps Mitch, he was very much a loner.

He wasn't unhappy. He'd never felt he was missing out until he'd met her and now he didn't know what to think. No, that wasn't true. He knew he'd found the part of him that was missing. The thing he couldn't understand was her. She was looking after him better than any partner and yet there was this armour-plating she'd erected since Polruan and he hadn't a clue how to smash through. If only she'd speak to him about the important stuff…

'How do I look?'

He'd been so wrapped up in his own thoughts he'd missed her grand entrance, his eyes skimming over her with a widening smile. He'd expected black, of course he had. Okay, so he'd noted a slight deviation over the last couple of days with the introduction of colour but he hadn't let on. He'd already said too much on that score and, by the look of things, she was sorting herself out despite his comments.

His gaze travelled from her shining hair, restrained in an elegant coil at the bottom of her neck, and down the smooth silky column of green that shimmered in the light. 'You look beautiful.'

He wanted to say more but he knew she wouldn't allow it. Since they'd arrived, she'd only allowed him to kiss her on the cheek; any other physical contact was kept to a minimum. Yes, they shared a bed but a bed to sleep in. She set rules, rules he had to adhere to or she'd leave and that was something he couldn't allow. He'd do anything to keep her by his side, even marry her.

His brow wrinkled as the idea took hold. Yes. He'd propose and in New York, too, he mused, taking her elbow and leading her out of the suite and across to the elevator. He'd meet the press and then drag her off somewhere quiet, if there was anywhere quiet in New York at this time of year. Tomorrow was New Year's Eve, a time for new beginnings, so tomorrow he'd ask her to be his wife.

But perhaps he was approaching this all wrong, he puzzled, placing a protective arm around her waist as they walked into the heaving lift. He'd never proposed before and Central Park, sitting in the back of one of those horse-drawn carriages, sounded ideal. He smiled down at the top of her head, his smile quickly turning into a grin as his mind continued on its fantasy. They'd have a small wedding back in England just as soon as he could arrange a licence. But first he had to face the media.

The conference room at The Hilton was packed with standing room only.

He manoeuvred her into a quiet corner at the back while he wandered across to the small stage to take his place between Mitch and the medical director of the hospital as if he hadn't a care in the world. In truth, now he'd sorted out his love life, he didn't.

He poured a glass of water and, with a smile for Mitch, folded his legs under the table and waited for Mr Powell to do his stuff with the introduction before the questions began in earnest. Staring at the sea of faces he even recognised a couple from three months ago as he gritted his teeth and listened to the usual drivel about it being a great honour to welcome such an esteemed, world-renowned team blah, blah, blah. He'd heard it all before if not a hundred times then at least a dozen. All he wanted was to drag his wife-to-be away somewhere private…

'Lord Ivy, how does this surgery compare to the last one? You know, where the twins died?' The question, out of the blue like that, wasn't unexpected but the tone of voice certainly was, as he glanced down at the tall redhead with bee-sting lips he'd bet his pension cost a fortune.

'The outcome for one, or haven't you heard, Miss—?'

'It's Ms, actually,' she replied, starting to scribble something on her pad before meeting his gaze. 'And the outcome, it's a foregone conclusion, is it?'

'Nothing is a foregone conclusion, as I'm sure you know. The team did what they could under the circumstances...'

'Under the circumstances. What circumstances?' her tone sharp.

'Now, now. I think it's time for a question from someone else,' Mr Powell interrupted, only to pause as Oliver continued to speak.

'It's alright, Mark. I'm happy to answer, Ms—er. The operation would normally have waited until both babies were of sufficient strength but, if we'd waited, it would have been to the detriment of one twin, the weaker one.'

'So you risked everything to save the weaker twin and, in effect, risked the life of the stronger one. Just how does that work exactly?'

Oliver felt his blood pressure rise at the question but what could he say? She was right after all. If he'd waited, they'd have lost Oliver. The operation, even from the distance of four days, was 10 percent skill and 90 percent luck and somehow she knew it as the smirk of all smirks decided to take up residence on her face. If she was a bloke, he'd have called her out but there was nothing he could do.

'Ms—er, I'm sorry, I didn't catch your name,' Mitch leant across and smiled one of his deadliest of smiles.

'Carter.' Her gaze, almost against its will, scrolled up and down the burly frame of the man staring across at her, a small smile starting to hover on her lips.

Mitch had that effect on women, Oliver remembered, as he sat back in his chair and decided to enjoy the show. Ms Carter, for all her sudden preening and chest thrusting, didn't realise he was toying with her very much like a cat with a mouse. There was only one woman for him, and he'd married her.

'Do you perhaps have children, Ms Carter?' He only continued when she'd shaken her head. 'Well I do. In fact, I have twins, Adele and Megan - little pickles, both of them,' he added, his Irish drawl engaging smiles from everyone in the room, and sighs from anything approaching the female persuasion. 'As a father of twins, I wouldn't be able to choose which one I should save if disaster befell them,' his voice now as hard as the hardest rock. 'I love them equally and, God forbid, I'd have to leave that decision to the experts if ever such a thing came about. Lord Ivy made the right decision, both this time and last time. Yes, the outcomes were different but, in both cases, he made the right call and it's him and the parents that have to live with the consequences, not us sitting in our ivory towers playing chess with other people's lives. This isn't chess, Ms Carter. This isn't about selling papers or, indeed, wanting to appear on Oprah. Lord Ivy travels around the world doing what he does quietly and without fanfare. This, I can tell you, is an anathema to him. He needs to be left alone to do what he does best, which is saving lives.'

'That ole cow-bag. May her haemorrhoids have haemorrhoids and her lips explode,' Mitch said, his eyes lingering on her back as she sashayed out of the room, one hand glued to her phone, the other fluffing up her hair, no doubt for the benefit of the cameraman trailing along by her side. He scrunched up the piece of paper she'd pressed into his palm on the way past before stuffing it in his empty glass.

'Ha, Professor MM has struck again. I have no idea how you do it, my old friend. It must be something to do with that Irish accent. You'll be charming the birds off the trees next,' Oliver chortled, his eyes searching the crowd for Holly. If he'd found it tough standing there being grilled like a kipper, he couldn't begin to imagine how she must have taken it. He'd never get used to the media as long as he lived.

'It's the only thing about this business I abhor,' Mitch growled as he walked off the podium. 'You know what, mate? That first beer isn't going to touch the sides. Although I'll probably only have the one, mind. Love sick fool that I am, I've booked myself on the red-eye out of here tomorrow so I will be back to planet mayhem in no time.'

'You love it. Liddy has been the making of you.'

Mitch pulled him to a stop, his eyes now on Holly. 'Don't let this one slip through your fingers, Ollie. There's something special…'

'I know what you mean,' his gaze soft. 'And I'll try not to. Enjoy your beer. I have a date with a wonderful woman.'

'Is it always like this around you?'

'Like what?'

'Bedlam.'

He'd reached her side and, although he wanted to draw her into the biggest hug, he contented himself with placing his hand on her elbow as they walked towards the elevators.

'That woman with the lips, she was beastly to you. If it hadn't been for Mitch putting her in her place, I'd have quite merrily decked her. What a bitch.'

'She was only doing her job,' he said, trying not to laugh at the thought of Holly raising her voice, let alone her fist.

'She wasn't doing it very well,' her face tightening into a frown. 'And what was that all about with her and Mitch at the end? It looked like she passed him something...'

'You spotted that,' he drawled. 'She wanted some more of that Gaelic charm. Mitch isn't like that.'

'And what about you? Are you like that?'

'Me?' his hand stiffened where it rested on her elbow, his fingers curling up. 'It wasn't me she was inviting for a bedroom romp.'

'And if she had—?' her eyes staring back, her pupils darkening.

'And if she had, my answer would have been the same as Mitch's. But I'm no saint, Holly. When a woman is foolish enough to fling herself at a man sometimes the inevitable is going to happen.'

'So, it would be her fault then, not the man's? She'd do the chasing and the outcome, even if the man was married and foolish enough to accept, would be all her fault?' her words mirroring his.

'I didn't say that. Look, what's gotten into you all of a sudden? She wouldn't come onto me in a month of Sundays and anyway, I avoid women like that like the plague. She's bad news and Mitch knows it just as much as I do.' He turned her away from the lifts and started heading for the bar instead. 'Come on, let's join Mitch for a drink and then make some plans for tomorrow. I've never spent New Year's Eve in New York and I quite fancy seeing the sights.'

Chapter Seventeen

Holly was rarely angry. She never lost her temper and she couldn't remember the last time she'd snapped at someone. Even after what Kyle had done, she'd just walked away. And when she'd met him that last time, on the day the annulment was finalised, she'd again chosen the path of least resistance and walked away. But now she was angry and not just angry…

She was devastated. Her whole world, the world that she'd known ever since arriving in London was now meaningless. He'd blame her or he would blame her when he found out. It would have all been her mother's fault - her mother; the home-wrecker, the marriage breaker, the woman that had come between his parents. Her mother, the woman that his father had left the property to and finally…her mother; the reason they couldn't be together.

The tears were streaming thick and fast but she didn't pause in her packing to brush them off her cheek. There was no sense or pattern to her reasoning. She didn't dwell on the fact that if her mother hadn't met his father she would never have met Oliver; his son. It was all too painful, too horrible for thought.

With one quick look around the room, she grabbed her bag and made for the door.

She'd left him with Mitch; one beer quickly turning into two. She'd blamed tiredness, exhaustion even and that wasn't a lie. She was so tired but not just physically. She pulled the door behind her and chose, in her wisdom, to take the stairs just in case she met him on the way down. She was running away but it was the only option for her at that moment. She'd have to meet him at some point but not now, now she wanted solitude and tears. She'd drown in her own self-pity if she could…

She had to get away but to where? She couldn't go home because he'd track her down. It wasn't as if he'd have any difficulty, all he'd have to do was ask the concierge.

Waiting at the airport was a nightmare, every look, every glance was one taken over her shoulder to check he hadn't followed. She didn't wait for the next flight to London, she couldn't risk it. She took the next flight available, which just so happened to be to Amsterdam. But it would do. Anywhere would do as long as it was away from him.

Standing, waiting behind the queue of people being directed to their seats the one thing she didn't realise - the one truth in all this. She could run away from him, she could put thousands of miles between them. But she couldn't run away from herself.

She'd never been to Amsterdam and she didn't go now. There would be a time in her life for tulips and trams but now wasn't it. She went straight through Customs and across to the British Airways Desk where she booked the next available flight to London.

London, as to be expected at this time of year, was cold and bleak, the snow now only a memory. Arriving at the station she threw a quick glance at the taxis. She'd love to go home and soak in the bath but the ever-looming threat that he'd find her was just too great.

She had enough clothes to be going on with. She had money and she even had her phone. That's all she needed as she headed for the underground and then the station to wait for the next train heading to Berkshire.

Wraysbury hadn't changed despite the fact she hadn't been back since her father's funeral eighteen years ago. The small, sleepy riverside village remained almost intact to memory and here, deep in the heart of the English countryside, slight traces of snow still lingered along the riverbank. But she wasn't here to take a trip down memory lane. She was here on a fact-finding mission, not that she expected to be able to find anything out after all this time. However she owed it to both herself and to Oliver to at least try.

She didn't know where to stay when she arrived. There was always a travel lodge or one of the larger hotels but at the back of her mind was still the feeling that he might try to follow. She couldn't remember what she'd told him about her childhood, and if she'd even mentioned Wraysbury, but she couldn't risk it. So, instead of a hotel, she chose a little scenic guesthouse called Corner Cottage conveniently tucked away down a quiet lane but within walking distance of the main street.

New Year's Eve night found her curled up by the window of her blue and white bedroom reading her mother's letter for the umpteenth time, not that it told her anything different. The only sentence that mattered was the one where she stated Holly's father was the Earl of Worton and therefore, by implication, that she was Oliver's sister. She could even be his twin sister in some freaky altered reality; after all they had the same father and very, nearly the same birthday.

Just like any successful businesswoman, Holly had already planned out the next couple of days as best she could. The first thing she did was to get in touch with Clare and inform her she'd decided to take a holiday with immediate effect. Of course, Clare wanted to know why her diligent and hard-working boss, who'd only ever taken one annual leave day ever, had suddenly decided to go wild. She suspected a man and, in a way, she was right.

Holly couldn't afford to go anywhere near Holly Branch Interiors because that would be the first place he'd look. She felt like a criminal on the run from the authorities or worse, but she just wasn't ready to see him yet. In truth, she'd never be ready. She was sorely tempted to let Clare in on the secret, not all of it, just enough to help her keep Oliver at bay - but this was a problem she couldn't discuss with anyone. Tomorrow, she'd chase up Kyle and Shirley and the day after, Mr Pidgeon should be back to work.

It had been easy to find Kyle in the end. All she had to do was ask at the guest house and she was given directions to a mock Tudor residence complete with rustic blackened beams and whitewashed walls. Everything was flash, brash and typical of him, even down to his fluorescent green sneakers and too-tight football shirt, straining across his flabby girth.

'Look what the cat's dragged in, I would say you're a sight for sore eyes but you're far too skinny.' Kyle smirked, his eyes lingering on her chest. 'I like my fleshpots fleshy, if you get my meaning?'

'I only wish you'd told me that before I married you.'

'That's your loss, love,' he sniggered, shouting over his shoulder to someone in the background. 'Come here, Tracy and meet the former Mrs Branch. I'd like to introduce you to Tracy, my fiancée and the love of my life.'

'I'll bet she is,' she mumbled through clenched teeth. 'A little young for you, don't you think?'

She studied the girl in front of her. She couldn't really call her a woman being as she looked about sixteen; a very busty sixteen-year-old but still only a child in her scruffy jeans and One Direction t-shirt.

'She keeps me young,' he said, slapping her bottom.

'Yes, well I'm not here to talk about your love life. In fact, it's really Shirley I've come to see if you could tell me where she is?'

'What, going to make reparations after all this time? I think it might be a little too late for that, don't you?' he said, his jovial smile changing in an instant. 'She was like a mother to you. For you to go and do the dirty on her when you weren't even his daughter…'

'Excuse me?' her face blanching.

'You heard. Everyone around here knew about your mother's little affair except you. Your mother was a scrubber and your father was mad to keep you after he threw her out; another man's leftovers. You make me sick. And, no, I won't tell you where Shirley is,' he added, slamming the door in her face with a final flourish.

She wandered back down the drive to the waiting taxi in a daze. All this time she'd taken heart from the fact her father, her real father, had never known she wasn't his daughter and yet here was Kyle telling her the exact opposite. Either her mother had lied in her letter or Kyle had lied – he'd said he was going to get even with her; he just had.

She couldn't believe how nervous she'd felt at the thought of meeting him, the man she thought she'd end up spending her life with and now…and now she felt nothing except perhaps pity for the girl he'd hitched himself to. It was as if history was repeating itself and there was nothing she could do to change it.

'Hey, wait up a minute.'

Holly heard the words but took a minute to realise that they were being shouted at her. Turning, one hand on the door handle, she was surprised to find Tracy standing by the gate looking anxiously over her shoulder.

'Did you want to speak to me?' She walked towards her, a gentle smile on her lips. For all Kyle's faults she felt nothing but sympathy for the girl rushing up to her.

'He'll kill me, but I couldn't have you thinking that him and me…that I'd…he's old enough to be me dad,' she muttered finally, her eyes resolutely staring at her scruffy trainers. 'He disgusts me, but I need the work.'

'It's alright,' she said, holding open the door and gesturing for her to get inside. 'Have a seat for a minute out of the cold, unless you have time for a coffee?' her eyes questioning. 'There used to be a little place on the High Street if it's still there…'

Ten minutes later found them sitting opposite each other with a coffee and a plate piled high with cream cakes, not that Holly ever ate anything resembling a bun or a slice of gateau. But to ease the situation, she chose the plainest, smallest confection before placing her elbows on the table.

'So my ex-husband isn't, that is, you're not engaged?'

'Am I hell!' Tracy said with a snort. 'He pays me to clean every Tuesday and Friday, that's it.' She paused, her eyes and then her fingers choosing the largest, creamiest eclair before continuing. 'He saw you from the upstairs window and offered me a hundred quid if I'd pretend to be his bird for like five minutes.'

Holly watched in amazement as she returned the half-finished bun to the plate with a wry smile before reaching under her t-shirt and pulling out a couple of rolled-up socks. It turned her from a blousy strumpet, in the making, to a very sweet teenager.

'It was all meant to be a gag, me pretending to be older and quite a bit larger,' she carried on as if nothing had just happened. 'But I didn't realise you were his wife – he never said. I wouldn't want to cause any trouble between you.'

'Ex-wife, Tracy,' her eyes twinkling as she glanced up from the rugby socks. 'Do you mind if I ask how old you are?'

'Nearly seventeen and, before you ask, I needed to leave school and get a job. It's not as if my foster mum and dad could afford for me to stay on, and I wouldn't let them. I'll get my education another way.'

I'm sure you will, she said, but not out loud. Instead she decided to bring the conversation back to Kyle. 'I hope he paid you before you agreed? He was a tight git when I knew him,' as she remembered the way he'd let her fork out for both the wedding and the honeymoon.

'I may be young but stupid I ain't,' she snapped back. 'Its money up front all the way with your husband,' she paused. 'Ex-husband. He's tighter than a duck's…'

'Yes, well, quite,' Holly interrupted quickly. 'So you wanted to tell me something perhaps; something about Kyle?'

'Yes,' she had the grace to blush. 'I wasn't eavesdropping but I heard what he said to you, I couldn't help it.'

'Of course not. In a way that's why I've come. But I wanted to see his mum, Shirley…'

'You'll be lucky.'

Holly hunched forward, both the coffee and cake now forgotten as she stared into the make-up-free face of the girl in front of her. She was so eager to find her now, someone she hadn't thought of in years, and this girl was her only link. 'Oh, why's that?'

'She's always steaming, is why. When Kyle threw her out, she got a job behind the bar at the Duke and Whistle and me foster-mother says it's all gone downhill for her. She lives in a flat over,' she added, starting to pick the marzipan off the top of a slice of Battenberg before nibbling with little white teeth. 'He's always asking me to deliver her post on me way home.' She picked up what was left and popped it in her mouth whole before pushing her chair back. She'd managed to eat more cake in five minutes than Holly had eaten in the last five months, not that she begrudged her even a crumb as she caught the eye of the waitress and paid the bill.

Watching her walk out the door, her head bowed against the wind, Holly was suddenly reminded of another young girl living in Wraysbury all those years ago. What she wouldn't have given for some motherly advice then, not that she'd have followed it. Just like Tracy, she'd thought she known it all. She'd known nothing.

'Can I drop you off somewhere, I've asked the taxi to wait?'

'I don't think so. He probably spotted me talking to you anyway so I'm pretty sure I've been sacked.'

'So, what are your plans then? A hundred quid won't go far.' They stared at each other in silence as the wind and then the rain whipped around them. Holly wasn't used to dealing with kids, and teenagers were like an alien species. But, for some reason she was probably going to regret, she wanted to help. Tracy had gone out of her way to do her a favour and had lost her job in the process. The very least she could do was try and make it better.

'What I mean is, I've been thinking of getting my assistant some help. She's far too overworked as it is. So, if you fancy moving up to London to become my assistant's assistant I can put you up in my spare room for a bit until you've sorted out a place of your own?'

Clare was going to kill her but it was true she'd been moaning about the long hours and Tracy, for all her belligerent ways and scruffy appearance could just be the answer. She just hoped she didn't live to regret sharing, what was after all, her private domain, with anyone, least of all a teenager.

If only there could be as happy an outcome from her meeting with Shirley, but that was never going to happen. For a start, she hardly recognised the scrawny woman opening the door with a belligerent moan about the time.

Shirley had always been a larger-than-life figure with her Marilyn hairstyles and bright red lips but a life of hard knocks, fags and beer had wreaked the worst kind of havoc and devastation on both her face and her body. She still had the hair but now it was in the form of a wig thrown haphazardly across the sofa like some stylised micro-pup to the stars. She also still had the lipstick-smeared lips but now the red bled into the deep-cut grooves in a parody of her famed trout pout. But it wasn't just her looks. She'd always surrounded herself in a cloud of Chanel Number 5, her signature scent. Now, in her grubby housecoat, with fag burns trailing across the front, she smelt of stale beer and sweat.

'What do you want? Come down here to gawp at the locals, have you?'

She restrained the barbed retort on her tongue, and instead, followed her through the door and into the small lounge. Shirley had never been the tidiest of people even when she'd moved in with Holly's super tidy father. But now the lounge bore all the marks of her deteriorating lifestyle. The flat would have been fine, not the largest she'd ever seen but a good space nevertheless with windows looking out onto a small courtyard. However, with nearly every surface littered with the day-to-day detritus of her life, everything looked dingy and decidedly unclean.

Shirley didn't even bother to offer her a chair before launching herself into the only clear seat, which happened to be a narrow sofa and there was no way Holly would feel comfortable sitting beside her.

'So, spit it out - what are you here for?' she said, reaching out a hand for her fags before lighting up. 'It must be something important for you to come traipsing all the way from London,' her eyes now on her face.

'It's about dad. Kyle said something...'

'You've been to see that moron of a son of mine,' she interrupted, her voice harsh. 'Bloody ingrate. He kicked me out and after all I've done for him.'

'Look, Shirley, I really don't want to go into all that.' She walked over to the window and absentmindedly picked up a photo from the pine chest of drawers underneath. 'I know you and my dad were fond of each other,' her eyes examining the happy couple on their way out to some dance or other.

'He was the love of my life, not that anybody believed me at the time. It was difficult enough with Kyle and then you; difficult for everyone. Everyone thought I was only after his money, as if he had that much. If I was going to go after money I'd have set my cap at a millionaire and not some two-bit antiques dealer,' she snapped, squashing her cigarette into the overflowing ashtray.

'Yes, well, it was all a very long time ago. I wanted to ask you about my mother,' she said warily 'I've learnt something...'

'What, about you being illegitimate? Your father never wanted you to know. As far as he was concerned, he was your father. After all, he was married to your mother when she fell pregnant...' her brow pulled into a frown. 'Who told you?'

'Nobody really, it just sort of came out. She died recently and there was a cottage...'

Shirley stood up then and joined her at the window, reaching out for the photograph. 'We were never going to be friends you and me but I was never your enemy, Holly. I never wanted you and Kyle to get together, you must know that? For all my many faults, I do know what my son is, and you're worth more than him. Your father loved you more than anything,' her hand touching her arm briefly. 'I don't know about your real father, it was before my time and it was something your father would never talk about, but it didn't make one jot of difference to him. He loved his first wife enough to let her go, and he loved you enough to keep you, even though he was only borrowing you.' She heaved a sigh, her eyes suddenly over-bright. 'Go away with you now and leave me in peace, I've a lot of clearing up to do before I start work.'

'Are you alright for money and stuff?' She watched as Shirley returned the photo frame to the windowsill, adjusting it slightly before answering, her gaze never wavering from Holly's dad.
She realised then that she'd made assumptions about Shirley, assumptions that were hard to overcome. She'd

always known, deep down, just how much they'd meant to each other. Kyle was a prat but his mother; his mother was alright.

'I'm fine, dear. I have somewhere to live and a job now.' She met her eyes, a small smile hovering on her lips before dropping her gaze. 'You just go out there and be a success. Some grandchildren would be good, that miserable git of a son of mine isn't going to give them to me.'

Arriving outside the offices of Messrs. Pike, Pidgeon & Prue for the second time in a week felt like twice too many. Holly was under no illusions that Mr Pidgeon would actually be in at eleven am on New Year's Eve, but that's all she knew.

'I'm so sorry, Mrs Branch that I can't offer you a coffee. My secretary is off now until next week and working the new percolator isn't one of my key skills,' he said, sitting behind his leather-bound desk and propping his elbows on the table. 'Now, what can I do for you?'

'I've been to see the cottage. It's lovely. But I do have some questions.'

'Ah,' he said, peering over the top of his bifocals. 'I thought you might. Just bear in mind that, whilst I was your mother's solicitor I was also your father's and therefore, I can't divulge anything that might be a clear conflict of interest.'

'Which one?'

'You have been busy.' He smiled briefly. 'I was solicitor to all three as it happens although; if your real father hadn't died I would have had to have done something about it.' He took off his glasses and, pulling a snowy, white handkerchief from his top pocket, proceeded to clean them. 'So what would you like to ask me?'

'It seems that I'm related to Lord Ivy, Lord Oliver Ivy that is.?'

'You know him?' his voice sharp, his eyes even sharper as they flickered at her from behind his sparkling lenses.

'Yes, we met—er—recently.'

'And Lord Ivy, he knows that you're his sister?' He threw her a shrewd look before continuing. 'No, I can see by your expression that he doesn't. Well, that must have put the cat amongst the pigeons, excusing the pun. Of course, you do realise you don't have any claim on the estate?'

'That's not why I am here,' she retorted, her eyes glinting.

'No, of course it isn't. But it has to be said all the same. As Lord Ivy was born within wedlock...It's all a muddle I must say, although lawyers are able to sort out most things...'
    'I don't think you're going to be able to sort out this one, Mr Pidgeon,' her voice now a thread of sound. 'If only we'd known before.'
    'I see.'
    'Can't you tell me anything...?'
    'Your father, your real father, Lord Ivy, came to me in despair.' Mr Pidgeon picked up his pen and started doodling on the blotting paper in front of him. 'He'd just found out that his wife and his mistress were with child. His first wife, the current Lord Ivy's mother, was fragile and he knew he couldn't leave her so...'
    'So, he left my mother to cope by herself.'
    'Now, you know that's not quite right, my dear. He provided for your mother, right up to her death.' He spread his hands wide. 'That's all I can tell you. That's all I know. Theirs was a great romance doomed to fail almost from the start. But I knew he loved her just as I know how much your father, both of them, loved you.'

***

Bother, bother, bother.
    He couldn't wait for her to leave and, as soon as he heard the outer door close behind her, he reached for the telephone.
    'Lord Ivy, Pidgeon here. We have a problem...'

Chapter Eighteen

Wraysbury
New Year's Day

New Year's Day and nothing to do. Normally she'd be at home in her black, silk lounging pyjamas working on her designs. Indeed, it was something she could still do but for some reason any enthusiasm for work had deserted her.

She had plans to pop over to see Tracy later to finalise arrangements but that still left the rest of the day.

'Everything alright, Mrs Branch?' Pauline Millward, the guesthouse owner, asked when she met her in the hallway. 'It's a beautiful day, cold and crisp - just right for a walk. One of the local houses is open this afternoon, if you're interested? I could make you a nice sandwich and a bowl of soup for lunch before you pop out again?'

Holly smiled to herself as she read between the lines. Mrs Millward was, in the most subtle way possible, telling her she didn't want her moping around the guest house all afternoon so she had two choices; staying in her room or doing as she suggested and visiting the gardens.

She followed her to the small reception area and watched as she rummaged through the drawers.

'Here it is,' she finally exclaimed, pulling out a flyer from under a pile of newspapers. 'Worton Abbey…'

'Worton Abbey? I think I've heard of that,' her voice soft.

'You may well have done. It's owned by Lord Ivy, not that he'll be there. He's never there. Some hotshot doctor. He only allows The Abbey to be open to the public once a year – it's a fundraiser in memory of his parents. They died when he was a boy, you know – such a tragedy. Here,' she added, pushing the dog-eared flyer across the desk. 'It's not far, about half a mile or so on from Saint Mary's Priory. In fact,' her eyes widening, 'you could always stop off, that's where the tree is; the tree where Anne Boleyn used to meet up with Henry the Eight.'

She never got to see the tree. In truth, she wasn't really interested in any 500-year-old love story where the, supposedly besotted, King ends up chopping off the head of his dearly beloved. She had too many problems of her own to be worrying about problems of the past as her long-suffering taxi driver joined the tailback waiting to turn in between the tall, ornate pillars that marked the entrance to Oliver's home.

The House had been rebuilt and now all that remained of the original Abbey was the gateposts. The current residence had fifteen bedrooms and eighteen bathrooms, a library and two lounges, as she read the leaflet that accompanied the entrance fee. There was also a grand hall, a dining room, the study and then the nursery with adjoining school room and not forgetting the games room, which was more than enough to be going on with. But, turning the page she also read about the servants' quarters and the kitchens and cellars, which were out of bounds to the tour.

She spent the next three hours traipsing up and down stairs in a maze to rival that of Hampton Court, determined over all else not to let the stiff back of the guide out of her sight. If she lost him, she'd never find her way out. Her skeleton would be found eventually in one of the many, dust-sheet covered rooms but it would probably take years because apart from Clare, Tracy and Pauline there was no one to give her absence a second thought.

There were also gardens innumerable and the recent addition of a sloping, Victorian-style gable-end greenhouse pinioned to the back provided an amazing backdrop for the delightful array of orchids on display.

She wandered around in a daze, all this beauty and splendour that would have been hers if only Lord Ivy's wife hadn't been pregnant with Oliver. Not that she begrudged him his inheritance. As far as she was concerned, he was welcome to it. The best thing would've been if they'd never met. And it was up to her to ensure that their paths never crossed again. She'd already decided to put the apartment on the market and, with the economy in London booming, she should at the very least be able to claw back the price she'd paid for it.

Standing to one side, she listened to the tall, bespectacled guide droning on about the original Abbey being raised to the ground after the dissolution of the monasteries by Henry VIII, who seemed to be popping up a little too frequently for her liking. She had nothing against history *per se.* On the contrary, as daughter of an antiques dealer she had a great deal of respect for anything old and unique. But, six-times married King Henry did little for her as she tried to remember how he'd gotten rid of his first five wives. There was that song she'd been taught in school if only she could remember it, a frown pulling between her eyebrows. It went something like; *divorced, beheaded, died, divorced, beheaded, survived…*

Almost tripping up the stairs, she paused a moment to glance over the bannisters and down at the Great Hall, resplendent with tapestry wall-hangings. If it had belonged to anybody else, she'd have loved spending time examining all the antiques on display. It was a beautiful house, although far from being a home. It needed children, lots of children chasing each other up and down the staircases as they played pretend battles through the large, roaming corridors. Instead of children's laughter there was a museum quality to the footsteps echoing across the highly-polished floorboards. She almost felt as if she was in church.

She finally found herself in the upper gallery surrounded by Gainsborough-type portraits, presumably of her newly discovered long-lost-relatives. And there at the end; a picture of her father and Oliver and, seated between them a raven-haired beauty, presumably Oliver's mother. Her father must've been around Oliver's age not that she could see any resemblance. He was tall, as tall as her father but where he'd been dark, this man had a delightful head of the fairest hair flopping across his forehead…

'Handsome man, your father.'

'Yes, very,' her response automatic as the words very much mirrored those running through her mind.

She paused, statue-still as she suddenly realised just who was standing by her side, his hand now on her arm.

She didn't want to move. No, that wasn't quite right. She couldn't move as all thought ceased except just one.

He knew.

Slowly, imperceptible she found herself turned in his arms, his hands now reaching up and encircling her shoulders, his gaze searching.

'How long have you known that...that you're my—?'

'Brother? Is that what you were about to say, Holly? I've known for a while, quite a while that...'

'Longer than you've known me?' she interrupted, her eyes never leaving his face.

She felt him sigh, his face suddenly flushed with colour. 'Yes, longer than I've known you, but it's not...'

But she wouldn't let him finish. Jerking backwards she stood facing him, her hands now on her hips. 'How could you? What was it, some kind of a joke or something? Let's see how far I can get with my little sis...' Her face paled, even as she raised her hand to her mouth. 'Oh, God. I think I'm going to throw up.'

Grabbing her by the arm he pushed her towards one of the doors marked private, which revealed a bright, light, golden room dominated by a huge, carved marquetry four-poster with sheer, golden voile drapes. But he didn't pause. Instead, he led her across the oak floor and into the bathroom.

'I'll wait outside.'

Splashing her face with water she stared up at the hollow-cheeked stranger looking back at her in the mirror. She'd lost weight over the last few days, which was always welcome, or usually so but now...now she realised just what a strain the last seven days had been, and the worst was yet to come.

She examined the room with a frown. There was no way out. He'd be standing outside the door, waiting – there was no escape. She glanced across at the mullioned window, its triangle panes glinting in the low, afternoon sun. She'd break her legs if she took that route, just a shame it wasn't a few floors up as broken legs wouldn't stop him.

Time was ticking and she knew she couldn't stay in there any longer so, with a final throwing back of her shoulders, she grabbed the door handle and pulled it open. She'd just leave, walk out on him. It's not as if there was anything he could either do or say to stop her. She didn't want a brother. Perhaps when she'd been five it would have been nice but now... no.

He was perched on the end of the bed, staring down at the floor and suddenly she wanted to go to him. She wanted to hug him to her breast and never let him go. But she couldn't do that. She'd never be able to touch or even see him again so, instead of doing what she wanted, she turned and made for the door.

'I've made a mess of everything,' his words echoed around the room and caused her to stop.

'It wasn't your fault, Oliver. Never think that, or that you're to blame. Our parents did a number on us. They put their own needs first with no thought as to the consequences.'

'Holly, you don't understand,' he said, standing up but remaining resolutely out of reach.

'What don't I understand, Oliver? That your father couldn't keep his hands off my mother? That he didn't give two hoots for my father, my real father? Be sure of this; your father means nothing to me.'

'He's not my father,' his voice soft.

Those words she'd been silently praying for were out, causing her knees to buckle. Reaching out a hand she pressed it up against her mouth before finally meeting his gaze.

'I don't believe you.'

'I'd hoped that you would but it doesn't matter now. It's too late. If only I'd told you...'

'Told me what? How can he not be your father?' her eyes widened as she suddenly thought of the beautiful woman standing so resolute beside her husband in that painting. If she'd been unfaithful too? But he was the Earl of Worton, wasn't he, her mind going into overdrive.

'I see you've finally worked it out,' his smile never reaching his eyes. 'Excuse me for not telling you earlier, but

I didn't learn myself until after their death and then only by accident.'

He stepped back and sank down onto the bed before patting the spot beside him. 'Come and sit down, Holly,' his eyes flickering to her face before returning to the floor. 'I promise I won't touch you,' he added, waiting in silence until she'd joined him.

'My parents, my beautiful parents weren't what they seemed. They were introduced at some dance or other and encouraged by their parents to make a match of it,' his hand snaking out, almost of its own volition and twining through hers. 'You know your father's part, probably more than I do?' his voice holding a question.

'My mother left a letter at the cottage.'

'Ah, I thought she might have,' giving her fingers a little squeeze. 'Well, my parents weren't so considerate. They told me zilch about anything. Right up to the time of—of the accident I thought that theirs was this amazing love match. He was so good to her, always bringing her flowers, chocolates, diamonds even. It was only later I realised it must have been guilt. We were staying in Switzerland for my fifteenth birthday when the avalanche happened, when my world came tumbling down around my ears and I stopped believing in fairy tales. I came off lightly at the time with only a smashed collar bone and a broken jaw for my efforts but for my parents...' He shook his head, his speech faltering. 'I was lying in hospital when some nurse or other strolled in and asked how she could get in touch with my father.'

'But, I don't understand...' she interrupted. 'How could—?'

'Remember, it was chaos; one of the largest avalanches ever to happen in that part of the world. My parents had been brought in, barely alive and they'd tried to save them but it was useless. They had no ID, it's not as if you take your wallet on the ski slopes,' he managed to laugh. 'We'd all needed blood transfusions and, that clever clogs of a nurse let slip that, whilst my mother and I had the same blood group it was, in fact, impossible for my father to have fathered me.' He lifted her hand onto his lap, their fingers still entwined. 'I have no idea who my real father is...'

'Well, I'll happily lend you one of mine, I seem to have picked up a spare along the way,' she managed, squeezing his fingers back.

He shifted, increasing the distance between them so he could turn and face her. 'You do know what this means, don't you?'

She shook her head, her vision blurring through the tears gathering momentum under her eyelashes.

'It means that all this is yours,' he said, spreading his hands. 'Worton Abbey and the money. As the rightful heir, you can take the lot.' He stood up then and, hands in his pockets, strolled across to the windows to gaze out on the lawns, now only a dim shape in the gathering twilight. 'I'll phone Mr Pidgeon in the morning and set the ball in motion.'

'But I don't want it.'

'It doesn't matter what you want, Holly,' his voice now harsh. 'It's too late for that. When you knocked on my window begging for a lift you set in motion a sequence of events that can't be halted. There's no definitive proof apart from those blood tests buried somewhere in some Swiss archive but that doesn't matter. Mr Pidgeon knows and he's such a stickler...'

'But if we go and see him? If we...'

'If we what, just tell him you're happy to lose out on millions of pounds of real estate? What if you marry, huh? What if your new husband takes a different view on things?'

'Well, will you?'

He frowned, a confused look on his face. 'Will I what?'

'Will you change your mind once we're married,' her face shining.

'I don't think I—?'

'Understand? I am surprised. I thought you doctors were all so brainy,' as she made her way across the room to join him by the window. 'Does it really matter if we're married, after all, the outcome is still the same?'

'The same?'

'Yes, my darling. We're only maintaining all this for our children anyway so it doesn't matter one jot which one of our names is on the title deeds,' she said, lifting up a tentative hand to his cheek. 'I quite fancy being a kept woman and, there's nothing wrong with the odd flower or chocolate...'

'What about diamonds?' sweeping her into an embrace before pressing his lips to hers.

'Well, one or two as long as it doesn't bankrupt us,' she said after a while, her hands now weaving through his hair. 'They'd be something to pass on to the girls.'

'Girls?' his eyes widening. 'Just how many are we planning on having?'

'Oh, two of each?'

'Two of each, that's four.'

'Correct, and here was me accusing you of not being very bright. We'll have four to start with, although I wouldn't object to a couple of more. How many bedrooms are there again?'

'Fifteen,' his voice faint.

'Fifteen might be a few too many. I'm not that young, after all. But we could always adopt, or foster come to that. Yes, why don't we do that...?'

He leant down and placed a kiss on the tip of her nose. 'You do know just how much I love you, don't you?'

'I bloody well hope so. I'm not going to all this trouble for just anyone, Lord Ivy.' She paused, her hand pulling gently on a lock of hair. 'So does this mean I'm a lady, even before the wedding then?' She paused, a little frown pooling, 'that reminds me, you haven't proposed.'

'No, I haven't have I, my lady,' his laugh ringing out across the room. 'And what a place to propose in, my darling,' as he bent down on one knee.

'Why, where are we?'

'The master suite. Now shush a minute. I've never proposed before so I need to think what I'm going to say.'

She felt a blush rip across her cheeks at the thought of that massive bed even as she struggled not to laugh at the look of concentration on his face. He'd be a wonderful husband and a wonderful father, she thought, as she watched him open his mouth and start to speak. She'd make him forget everything that went before by filling every corner of their home with the sound of laughter.

'Lady Ivy, may I have the honour of your hand in marriage,' he started, only to be interrupted by the feel of her lips as she knelt down in front of him.

'Yes, my darling. Now, that that's over, I do think we need to check the mattress. After all, I don't want to spoil the wedding night with backache from lumpy springs.' She giggled, reaching up and starting to unravel his tie.

'But, we should wait...' his eyes scrunching up. 'Don't you want to, you know—?'

'Really, Lord Ivy, you do need to work on finishing your sentences,' as she dropped the tie on the floor before starting on his buttons...

'But, but—?'

'But nothing, Ollie. If you expect me to become Holly Ivy,' she paused, her lips pulling into a wry smile. 'Well, I get to choose the time and the place and, after all the nights lying awake while you've snored your head off, it will be a nice change to have you both horizontal and awake for once,' she ended, leading him by the hand to the bed before shoving him down on the mattress and heading across the room to turn the key in the lock.

Epilogue

The Ballroom
Nettlebridge Manor
March 1st

'**F**our orange juices and 4 pints.'

'For God's sake don't get them mixed up, Matti,' Pascal declared, his eyes brimming with laughter as he reached for Sarah's hand under the table. '*Jus d'orange* is an anathema to a Frenchman.'

'As if I'm likely to forget,' he said, starting to hand out the glasses. 'More than my life is worth,' he added, throwing a wink across the table at Cara. 'We've already got the reputation for being the go-to-table for anything and everything baby talk as it is. Do you think that's why Lady Nettlebridge decided to seat all the pregnant women together, or was there another motive entirely? I have to admit to feeling slightly left out seeing as I'm the only commoner here. In fact, if I wasn't a lawyer I could get a complex about being in the company of an earl, a marquis and a viscount. If there's any disputes to be settled don't include me. You'll probably want to sort them out at dawn with pistols, or bows and arrows or something.'

'Hah, that's what you know; its pistols or swords. Bows and arrows are from the time of Robin Hood and Sherwood Forest,' Pascal drawled with a smile.

'And how would you know? You're French?'

'And you're American, but I won't hold it against you.' Pascal laughed. 'Is there a rule about Frenchman not been able to understand medieval English folklore?'

'It's called the Battle of Agincourt,' Tor interrupted. 'Now, enough you two. You'll have Ollie and Holly thinking we're a bunch of louts instead of respectable pillars of the community...' He paused at the sound of giggling coming from his left. 'And what's so funny about that?'

'You are, all of you,' Tansy managed, tears streaming down her face. 'Pistols at dawn, ladies, or should we just lock them out of our rooms tonight?' she added, throwing a smile across at Sarah and Cara.

'It's a little late for that, don't you think, my love,' his hand now pressed against her rounded stomach even as he started nuzzling her neck. 'About four months too late,' even as he threw a wink across at Holly. 'You'll have to excuse my wife, it's the hormones. Wait a few minutes and the other two will be at it, won't they lads?'

Holly just smiled, even as she felt Oliver squeeze her knee before resting his hand on her leg.

They'd only been back from their honeymoon a week when the invitation from Lady Nettlebridge was pushed through the letterbox. She couldn't very well decline even though she did wonder if the invite would've been forthcoming if she wasn't now Lady Ivy. Just because she'd redesigned the ballroom wasn't usually a reason to be invited to the ball.

Looking around the golden, fabric-covered walls and sparkling chandeliers, she was glad she'd managed to persuade her ladyship to discard the African theme for that of a traditional Tudor banqueting hall, which was far more in keeping with the 16th century Manor House. She viewed it as a farewell to arms in a way because it would be the last big interior decorating project she'd be able to manage. She was still a career woman, as she told Oliver that night at the abbey. She still wanted to work but now with her news…no, their news, still fresh in her mind, she decided she wasn't as career-minded as she'd previously thought, even as she lifted his hand and placed it over her still-flat abdomen.

It must've happened that first magical evening at the abbey because, after, he'd put his foot down and said they should wait until he'd put a ring on her finger. She smiled, her eyes snagging on the square-cut emerald he'd presented her with a crooked smile as if he was worried she'd hate it.

'Don't mind him,' Tansy interrupted as she pretend swatted Tor with her napkin. 'What I want to know is how you feel about nurseries, Holly?' She grinned. 'The nursery at Brayely Castle is a little mouldy...'

'Hey...' Tor interrupted, his eyes flashing. 'There's nothing wrong with mould.'

'Darling, you can have as much mould as you like but not near the baby, although I was thinking of a mural and there could be a mushroom or two?'

Holly laughed at the sight of them sparing gently over their drinks even as she felt an idea bud and bloom under the weight of the sudden looks of interest thrown at her by the other two women. There was a wealth of work in designing for children and, these would be small rooms, nothing like the grand scale of the ballroom, as her eyes travelled over the room's football-pitch proportions.

'I've been thinking of scaling things down at work a little,' she said, well aware of Oliver stiffening in his chair. She hadn't been thinking of any such thing but now she wanted to be by his side; she wanted to accompany him when he raced off somewhere to perform those miracles even as she thought about the pictures of baby Mitch and Oliver that had arrived in the post earlier. She wanted it all but she couldn't have it all. She couldn't have her cake and eat it, and now she had other people to consider.

Lifting her bag up she pulled out a notebook and scribbled down her details rather than giving out one of her business cards. This wouldn't be business. This would be a pleasure. Tracy was shaping up very well and, with Clare as a guide, there was no reason why the scaled-back business couldn't continue until she finally decided what to do with it.

'That's wonderful,' Tansy replied. 'And just to add, I'm nothing like my mother,' her eyes now on the silver-clad woman, bedecked in diamonds, tapping on her glass with a heavy hand.

'Thank God for that, I wouldn't have married you if you were,' Tor interrupted as they all turned in their seats to watch Cara standing up and making her way slowly to the grand forte piano stacked with candelabras, the red ball gown cleverly disguising her pregnancy from even the most discerning of gazes.

All eyes in the room now turned and conversation quietened as Lady Nettlebridge announced that the world-renowned pianist, Cara Bianchi had been persuaded to come out of retirement, but only for a special charity performance.

The notes of Chopin's Piano Concerto Number Two swelled and dipped, flowing over, around and through the air like a magician waving his wand. All was silent as the beauty of the room merged and intertwined with the beauty of the notes spinning out from Cara's mercurial fingers. She looked beatific, finally at peace with her new life.

'Are you happy, my love?'

'Never happier,' Holly whispered back, her arms nestling behind his neck as they swayed to the soft ballad being played by the band that had now replaced Cara. 'I can't believe last week we were still in Polruan on our honeymoon...'

'The honeymoon's not over yet,' his lips moving from her forehead to plant the sweetest kiss against her lips. 'Have I told you how beautiful you look in that gown?'

'Well, thank you, my lord,' as she stole a quick look at the yellow frock she'd chosen from her mother's stash of vintage dresses. 'There was little point in buying anything new... Goodness only knows what size I'll be after the birth.'

'Births, sweetheart.' A wicked grin stamped on his face. 'Two babies, two births.'

'Don't remind me.' she moaned. 'What is it with you lot and twins anyway? What with Mitch and Liddy, and now us... if I'd realised just what a stud I'd married, I'd never have agreed to...'

'If you might remember, Lady Ivy, it was you who jumped me, and I am only human after all. If it's on a plate, I'm going to eat it.'

'Shush, someone might hear...'

'As if they'd be interested in our conversation.' He threw his head back and laughed. 'We're a pair of nearly middle-aged old fogeys and, talking of age, I'm feeling a little jaded after all this excitement,' his eyes again drawn to her chest.

'Do you think we could slip away so I can have a little snooze?'

'Why didn't you say,' her voice now full of concern. 'I just knew you were burning the candle, driving up and down to The Abbey each day. It's too much, you know, far too much for a man of your age,' she reiterated, leading him over to the table so she could grab her bag and wish the other three couples a hasty goodnight.

On the short journey back to the house, he remained silent, resting his head back against the seat with his eyes closed only to open them when Parker pulled up in front of the door. She was worried, more than worried as she flittered around him very much like the anxious wife she was.

'Is it your head? I knew I should have made you go and see that specialist. What can I get you? Paracetamol? Or, what about a nice cup of tea?' She watched him sit down on the edge of the bed to take off his shoes before starting on his tie.

'Come here.'

'I am here,' she said, walking towards him. 'What is it? Do you have a pain?'

'More like an itch.'

'An itch?' her eyes widening. 'Where, can't you…?'

'It's not that sort of itch, Holly,' and she suddenly noticed the gleam in his eye.

'Oh. You old fraud. I was really worried.'

'How worried?' his hand flicking out and grabbing onto her wrist. 'Worried enough to kiss it better?'

'Now that would depend,' her lips twitching.

'On what?'

'On where it hurts, of course,' she added, allowing him to pull her down onto his lap, his hands working on her zip before slipping the fabric off her shoulders to pool at her waist.

'Well, it really hurts here.' He raised a finger to his left cheek, before pausing in consternation. 'In fact, it hurts all over. In fact,' his forehead now pulled into a frown. 'In fact, it's more of an ache than a pain or an itch; an ache just here,' his hand now over his heart. 'It's an ache that will never go away.'

'I have the same ache,' she whispered softly.

'Really?'

'Yes, and it's in the exact same spot,' as she raised his hand and placed it over her left breast. 'I have heard that there is a cure though.'

'Really,' he repeated, his head dipping towards her lips.

'Yes, really. It's not an immediate cure, you understand. In fact, I've heard it might take years, many, many years of treatment before there's any sign of improvement.'

'Well, the sooner we get started the better, don't you think?'

Words stilled as eyes, hands and lips took over the conversation.

The End

Acknowledgements.

Books don't get written by themselves. It needs a lot more than just a notebook and a biro to turn a blank page into a novel. For me it has taken 25 years, the length of time since I visited Polruan on our honeymoon. But the memories of that magical corner of Cornwall still linger....

Forever cottage is straight from my imagination but Polruan Stores is central to the community. Thank you, Kiki for your kindness.

Thanks also to both Pauline Millward and Clare Wakelin for letting me borrow your names – I hope you like your characters?

Also thanks to the busy members of my street team for putting up with a pre-edited version. I really appreciate all of your efforts. And talking about editing, a huge thanks to Natasha Orme, who has done an amazing job at whipping this manuscript into something fit for reader consumption.

Finally love, as always, to my three wonderful children for putting up with me…I promised the twins *twins* – I hope I managed!

Writing is an obsession but without someone to read my stories I wouldn't get very far so thank you - I love hearing from readers. You can find me on Twitter (not a lot) Instagram (occasionally) and Facebook (too much). I also have a website with links to all of the above, in addition to a newsletter link where you can sign up for information on special offers and competitions – jennyo@bravesites.com

Best wishes
Jenny O'B

25114095R00079

Printed in Great Britain
by Amazon